"There's no one you can call to let them know what we're doing?"

Darby wanted confirmation they were proceeding down the correct path.

"I don't trust anybody. Neither should you."

He heard her low, throaty growl of frustration. He closed his eyes again, trying to recall the handler's face who had set him up so thoroughly tonight.

Strangely enough, he could only picture Darby at the moment she chose to help him. The panic that flooded her eyes had been conquered and set aside with one determined heartbeat.

This woman was more than under his skin and he hadn't even known her a full hour.

ANGI MORGAN

.38 CALIBER COVER-UP

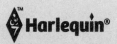

TORONTO NEW YORK LONDON
AMSTERDAM PARIS SYDNEY HAMBURG
STOCKHOLM ATHENS TOKYO MILAN MADRID
PRAGUE WARSAW BUDAPEST AUCKLAND

THANKS Devona...for Erren. Jill...whew, nine weeks. Amy, Carol,
Kim, Kym, Regina & Robin...there are no words thankful enough.
And Kourtney...we made it to Disney World!

Recycling programs
for this product may
not exist in your area.

ISBN-13: 978-0-373-69529-4

.38 CALIBER COVER-UP

ABOUT THE AUTHOR

Angi Morgan had several jobs before taking the opportunity to stay home with her children and develop the writing career she always wanted. Volunteer work led to a houseful of visiting kids and an extended family. College breaks are full of homemade cookies, lots of visitors and endless hugs.

When the house is quiet, Angi plots ways to intrigue her readers with complex story lines. She throws her characters into situations they'll never overcome...until they find the one person who can help.

With their three children out of the house, Angi and her husband live in North Texas with only the four-legged "kids" to interrupt her writing. For up-to-date news and information, visit Angi at her website, www.AngiMorgan.com.

Books by Angi Morgan

HARLEQUIN INTRIGUE
1232—HILL COUNTRY HOLDUP
1262—.38 CALIBER COVER-UP

CAST OF CHARACTERS

Dallas police officer Darby O'Malley—Until recently her only desire has been to work undercover. Now, it's to clear her younger brother of murder charges. She's on the edge of losing her job and her brother just might be guilty.

Undercover DEA agent Erren Rhodes—He's been undercover for six years and he's ready to get out before he makes a mistake and "gets dead." When his mentor is murdered, he's ready for justice.

Academy officer Walter Pike—Darby's partner asked Erren to deliver the package, but was murdered before he could leave instructions.

Assistant district attorney Brian Thrumburt—Pike told him this case would make his career.

DEA agent John Knighton—Erren's handler who disappears while watching Erren's back.

The sergeant major—Denny O'Malley, U.S. Army, retired, and Darby's father.

Sean O'Malley—Darby's older brother. The only O'Malley sibling with a boring desk job.

Michael O'Malley—His blood type was found at the scene linking him to Pike's murder. Shot and in a coma, he has all the answers, but no one can ask him the questions.

Chapter One

Alley. Lexus. Two drug dealers.

The situation read like a bad book: *The Auto-Frickin-Biography of Erren Rhodes*. He was pathetic. He would dread going through the motions of this meeting, but he was numb. Numb to the filth he dealt with on a daily basis. Numb to the filth he'd portrayed for the last six years. Numb to his filthy shell of a life.

Pike was dead and in the ground. Ambushed. Executed.

No witnesses.

Rhodes was certain no one had seen him at the funeral of his mentor, the man who had kicked his teenage years into shape. He'd stayed out of sight. He'd hung around the edges of the cemetery just as he did the edges of his fictional existence.

It was a dark and stormy night...blah, blah, blah. He'd laugh if it weren't playing out in front of him like a colorized black-and-white film. It was time to get out of deep-cover work, but not before he found Pike's murderer. He wouldn't let the bastard go without justice.

Unfolding his legs, he climbed from the rundown rental he'd taken for the op. His first mistake. He should have insisted on something flashy like the sweet SUV at the end of the alley. Second mistake? This dark real estate. Drug deals went down at steak restaurants. Always in public places. So why was this meet for information set like a bad flick?

Backlit by the car's headlights, two men came at him, arms extended, guns aimed at his chest. This was *not* the plan.

"You dudes have been watchin' too many movies." Yeah, he was mouthing off like a street thug—something he shouldn't do but couldn't help. He knew the drill and placed his hands at the back of his neck when Beavis and Butthead stepped closer. "Holdin' the barrel sideways like that, empty casings can hit—"

"Shut up, fool." The gold-toothed, eyebrow-pierced Butt-head took another confident step closer.

Six years ago adrenaline shoved him to recklessness. Now it didn't register. All these guys acted the same. Digging in with pond scum required a dedication he no longer had. His Dallas handler waited around the corner. Like he needed backup for this two-bit op? He could do this in his sleep.

Butthead shoved the barrel of a .357 Magnum under Rhodes's chin while patting him down.

"You don't talk 'til we says you talk," the bleach-blond Beavis barked, nervously shifting from one foot to the other in front of the rental.

Nodding, despite the barrel rammed into his Adam's apple, Rhodes let them think they were in charge. Two bad-ass-wannabes who didn't know him from Jack. Butthead lifted Rhodes's gun from its shoulder harness under his Ed Hardy jacket and dropped it into his pocket. His eyes never met Rhodes's straight on.

Flashy guns and jewelry, designer-label clothes and a Lexus. Not the ordinary run-of-the-mill street crap he'd been led to believe he'd be dealing with. Rhodes's nostrils flared at the cloying scent of heavy French cologne floating through the smell of old garbage. Did he have the right guys? They sure seemed to know *him* since two barrels pointed straight toward unprotected parts he'd like to keep.

Shake it off. Nothing was wrong. He'd done this before. First-meet jitters. That was it. Yeah, that crappy feeling in the pit of his stomach had nothing to do with Beavis or Butt-head and everything to do with the drive-through burritos for dinner.

"Get in the car," Butthead demanded.

Rhodes stiffened. "No one said anything about a ride. I have the money in my backseat." He came to conduct a small exchange of money for information. These punks were some-how connected to Pike's murder and he was close to finding a serious lead to seal the coffin on the creep they had in custody. But that slippery grin behind the gun wasn't the normal evil he faced every day.

These guys looked nervous, high and prepaid…

Damn.

"Do what you're told," Beavis yelled in a crazy-high voice.

"What's wrong, man? I got the cash." Rhodes searched his right, hunting Dumpster locations. Butthead shoved the pistol barrel in his back again, pushing him toward the Lexus. No way was he getting in that SUV.

"Get your ass in the car." Butthead circled the barrel of the gun in the air. "Get in!"

This op might get his blood pumping after all.

Rhodes shook his head. "What's up, man? I'm only pickin' up a package." Getting in that car would be the last thing he ever did.

"You got that wrong, dipwad. You're deliverin' tonight," Butthead said, hissing a laugh between clenched teeth.

Cryptic messages were not a good sign. With one step, Butt-head had cut him off from his car. That sealed it. He'd been set up. What would they want with him? Or was someone trying to push him out of the picture? These guys had answers and he had lots of questions. A different dread took over his body. His mind released its hold on his tensed muscles. Everything automated, ready for a fight.

Patrol lights flashed at the end of the alley. Butthead froze. Wrong move. Spinning, Rhodes lifted his leg and let his worn-out Air Jordan knock Butthead's gun behind the strip mall's Dumpster.

Butthead wasn't going down without a fight. Rhodes didn't want to go mano-a-mano, but he threw a punch to Butthead's chin. The man dodged, dipped his shoulder and gave a blocking tackle to make any football coach proud. Right into Rhodes's gut.

Air whooshed from his lungs as they crashed to the ground, splashing water from a pothole. Bright bits of light flashed across his briefly closed eyes. Thrusting the big goon off, he kicked out, catching the perp's face. His shoe should have knocked the living daylights out of the goon.

Butthead sat up, spit out his gold cap and grinned.

Rhodes caught sight of Beavis's weapon waving around, attempting to follow their rushed movements. A bullet pinged off the rental car behind him. Then Beavis dove behind the Lexus's car door and fired a couple of rounds toward the lights.

Rhodes squinted into the blinding floodlights, expecting his backup. *Who was shooting? Why weren't the cops demanding they drop their weapons?*

Ricochets sent him scrambling for cover as a sudden surge of bullets peppered the broken asphalt. Beavis crawled into the Lexus, kept his head down and backed up, leaving rubber in the potholes. One of the patrol cars quickly pursued him around the corner.

Rhodes couldn't make it to his car and turned toward his alternate exit, but Butthead jumped him from behind. Even with the unknown gunmen firing shot after shot, this stupid dog wouldn't let go of his bone—which just happened to be Rhodes's neck.

He recoiled from Butthead's blood-speckled face and fetid breath, but the solid pressure against his throat was making things fuzzy. With no other choice, he pushed his fingers into Butthead's eyes. There was a growl in Erren's ear and a rush of air into his lungs. The rapid fire around their heads had him wincing. He wanted this guy alive and talking. He wanted to stop the cops from shooting, but had little chance to catch his breath as he stumbled backwards.

"Give it up, man. It ain't worth losing our lives," Rhodes shouted. It really wasn't. And right now those cops didn't know he was one of the good guys.

Butthead pulled a switchblade, popped it open and charged. Rhodes grabbed the giant's wrists, keeping the blade inches away. They went down a second time. Rolling over. Then back. Every rock jabbed into Rhodes's bruised, sore body. The knife was between them. Then somehow pointing under Rhodes's chin.

Desperate, he pushed Butthead's hands further south. Butthead outweighed him by fifty pounds and the searing pain along his side proved that the bigger man had gained the upper hand.

"Aarrggh!" God, he was on fire. The expectation of the blade tearing his flesh again was worse than knowing he'd been double-crossed. His hands shook while he kept Butthead from twisting the handle and slicing his insides to shreds.

The blade slowly and painfully slid away.

A car window exploded above him. Butthead's body blocked most but not all of the glass. He cringed, giving Rhodes the split-second chance he needed. He threw Butthead off and rolled to a crouch.

Butthead leaped to his feet. A bullet whizzed by Rhodes

and hit his adversary straight in his heart. A flower of blood blossomed over Butthead's shirt and he fell to his back.

"Don't shoot!" Rhodes threw up his hands and faced the flashing lights. He quickly brought his left arm back down to his injured side.

Another round whistled past. Son of a… Who was shooting from above and behind him? The cops returned fire, leaving him caught in the dead zone. Any rookie could tell a man was down and his hands were empty. What more did they need?

He'd sort through the explanations later. Rhodes ran to Butthead and searched for his gun. He found an envelope. Maybe this was the evidence he needed.

The rented Honda hatchback was perforated with holes and lacked a passenger window, but he didn't need to drive it far. He punched the gas, heading through the alley onto the deserted street.

Completely deserted. No Drug Enforcement Agency backup in sight. Maybe he was the lone shooter? Just what he needed, confirmation he was on his own. But his priority was to stay alive.

He pressed the pedal to the floor, turning several corners to evade anyone following. The only thing he'd done right was stash his Suzuki four blocks away. He ditched the rental in a parking garage and avoided cameras on his way out of the building.

Up to his neck in alligators. Totally on his own. His gut told him not to follow protocol, ditch everything familiar. Someone wanted him to lay off Pike's case. His stomach rolled and his side throbbed. He reached down and a warm stickiness oozed through a jagged hole.

"Man, he ruined my favorite Ozzy shirt."

Pulling the lock from the wheel of his cycle, he straddled the bike and tore open the envelope. Inside was a photo of Pike with an unknown man. On the reverse was a hand-drawn map, some scribbles and instructions from his mentor for a meeting that should have happened three days ago.

Things were getting more dangerous by the minute.

Interesting.

DARBY O'MALLEY STARED at the freshly painted and very blank white walls. Blank. And white. She appreciated the simplicity of the unadorned space. Perhaps because nothing in her life could ever be simple. And it didn't help that her decorating talents sucked.

"White? You need to brighten this place up." Her brother Sean smiled while complaining about the lack of color. "I saw some purple fuzzy pillows at Grapevine Mills Mall that would look great. Or maybe some orange frames for all those pictures you had me haul in here last week. Or maybe neon-pink flamingos. Nothing red though—we don't want to clash with your hair."

Her hair wasn't red. At least not O'Malley red. She paid good money to add those "natural" highlights. The teasing had lasted throughout the entire fix-up day and continued through the Mexican food and beer that night.

Brothers were supposed to do that. Right? Be intrusive and try to repair more than the broken items around your house. She should know. She had three very intrusive O'Malley brothers and a sergeant major for a dad.

Darby appreciated Sean's desire to play best friend, but this particular problem couldn't be fixed over a couple of Coronas. They hadn't spoken about their brother lying comatose in a hospital bed inside a lockdown ward. They couldn't visit. Couldn't help him recover.

She needed to be by herself. Away from a dad who barked orders, and the brothers who followed them.

Finally living on her own at the age of twenty-six. Finally no roommate to eat her favorite cereal. Finally no dirty dishes in the sink except her own. She was more than ready. And no one understood. She hardly understood it herself. She'd lived with someone since college and tolerated way-out-there tastes. Purple was not her favorite color. She wasn't even certain she *had* a favorite. Weird. She'd never given it much thought before.

This was a new beginning. A time for new goals. But not the time of night to unpack boxes of old memories.

Tonight, it had taken an hour and her promise she'd come by Sunday before Sean would leave. As far as her brothers were concerned, there wasn't a problem in the world that couldn't be solved over a Cowboys game and a grilled steak.

If only their brother Michael's problems were that simple.

"Michael will wake up and I'll clear his name." She had to. She was a cop. A cop whose brother had been accused of murder. Talk about your conflicts of interest.

A thump interrupted her nightly pity party. She hit the mute button on the remote, hoping it was a sound effect from the old Lon Chaney movie on TCM. Nope, there it was again. She crossed the new carpet and tile, looked through the very unsafe, four-paned back door and didn't see a thing. She shrugged, took a step back and heard another whack on wood.

The back porch's light lit the entire deck. No one stood on the other side of the triple locks. At least not that she could see. She slid her hand into her holster on the counter and pulled her Glock from its resting place. She'd chosen this neighborhood in North Dallas because of the low crime rate, but someone could think she was an easy mark. Not likely.

And then again, the kids across the street were famous for their practical jokes. She'd heard all about them the day she'd moved in. Just what she needed…a neighborhood of pranksters. If she barged out there as if she was on a drug bust, she'd probably scare those children directly into therapy.

So don't overreact.

There it was again. A solid bump on the deck. Kids or no kids, she wasn't going anywhere without her Glock pointed straight ahead.

She should call the local P.D. and teach those kids a lesson. But then she'd have every parent on her back for as long as she lived here. And the last thing a new owner needed was trouble with the neighbors.

No way. She was a trained police officer. She could handle a couple of kids. So what if she scared them with the gun?

It was after eleven. How had so many hours passed since she'd gotten off work? Still dressed in her uniform right down to her shoes. Well, at least she'd changed her shirt when Sean had come over.

Squinting through the lacy curtains the previous owner had left, she now saw a shadowy figure lying on the steps. With her eyes on the body, she quickly unlocked and opened the door. Darby stepped outside and scanned the shadows in the tiny backyard. No potential threats. Nothing. He seemed to be alone.

"Police. Don't move," she said, aiming her gun at the suspect.

A man—not a kid—was slumped across the steps. Moonlight shone on a beard-stubbled face and long, dark hair.

"O'Malley?" His head thudded against the wood. "Need… help."

Okay, so he wasn't some random nutcase. He'd asked specifically for her.

"Why do you want O'Malley?" *Why hadn't she brought her cell outside to call 911?* She continued to hold the man at gunpoint, but he didn't look as if he was going anywhere.

His breathing was shallow and ragged, his eyes were closed and he held his side as if he was injured.

"Gotta stay a...wake."

"Who are you?"

"Pike said I could trust you," he panted. "Undercover. No... hospital." The last of his words faded as he appeared to slip into unconsciousness. His hand fell away, covered in blood.

"God almighty." Darby pushed her gun down the back of her pants and bent to her knees. She frisked him. He wasn't carrying a weapon, but there was a photo of Pike on a fishing pier. The reverse side had a map to her house and a coded message from her brother Michael.

Rolling the stranger to his back, she felt his chilly neck for a pulse. "Talk to me. What does this have to do with Michael? What trouble will you be in if I call an ambulance to save your hide?"

Baggy jeans and a black extra-large T-shirt helped disguise the blood seeping across his side. Good grief, she couldn't let him bleed to death on her back steps. He was soaked to the skin, with no jacket and an empty shoulder holster.

Was he here for the package? How could she be certain he was the person Pike mentioned? But Michael had sent him, so how did it all fit together?

"No docs," he mumbled. "Verify...two one four...five five five...nine six nine six."

Darby took one last look at the yard. No movement. It was the wrong thing to do, but she grabbed the unconscious stranger under his arms and pulled him through the door. He moaned, but didn't give any indication he was waking. She lowered him to the tiled breakfast nook floor.

God, what was wrong with her? She couldn't do this again. Just call 911 and deal with the repercussions later. Still thinking she shouldn't get involved, she knelt and yanked the Ozzfest shirt up to the guy's armpits.

Smooth, sculpted pecs and abs—make that an entire six-pack—would normally have her biting her lip to keep from drooling. But none of it mattered. A small knife wound, covered in blood, marred his left side. She pulled dishtowels from a kitchen drawer and placed them over his wound, closing her eyes.

Deep breath. In through the nose…out through the… Shoot, that only made it worse. The metallic smell of blood mixed with the leftover Chinese takeout on the counter invaded her senses. Her stomach flinched, forcing her memory to a place she didn't want to revisit.

There was no way she could deal with Pike's death now. But this guy had asked for her and had something to do with her murdered friend. There had to be someone she could call. She couldn't let the guy die.

That sealed it. She pulled her purse off the counter, sending quarters, dimes and eyeliner rolling across the floor. Her cell phone bounced once and popped the casing in two different directions. Her badge and lip gloss headed in two others. The man stirred.

"God," he moaned, his voice as deep as sin. "I passed out?"

He rapidly blinked lashes too long to be considered manly. Yet on him, they framed a pair of ancient amber-brown eyes. Her right hand kept the towels in place as her left slid around her hip and rested on her gun.

"Who are you and why can't I call a doctor?" she asked.

"Ah, crap. I'm going to puke."

"Terrific. As if bloodstained grout isn't enough." His stomach muscles contracted under the tips of her fingers as she heard the age-old accompaniment to dry heaves. Her own gag forced her eyes shut.

One second she was preparing to jump out of the way. The next her shoulders were pinned to the floor with the stranger straddling her hips, her gun in his hand pointed at the ceiling.

"Pike said you were good. The best," he said, too confident and boastful in his dominant position. "Well, except me. I need some help, O'Malley. Pike left a package for me, and I need it. Tonight."

"If you know who I am, then why are you sitting on me?" Faker. He wasn't the least bit woozy.

One jab in his wound and he'd be writhing on the floor. If he pointed the barrel toward her, she wouldn't hesitate. But there was something about him... Something that made her wait for his next move. Something other than Pike and Michael instructing her to trust him.

"I'm asking, politely, one more time."

"Ask any way you want," she answered.

The solid weight across her legs was uncomfortable. He eased his hand from her shoulder, scooping up the bloody dishtowels along the way. The moment of alarm at being confined lifted, and she could think again.

"I like you," he said, leisurely lifting one corner of his mouth in a smile. "Pike must have been out of his ever-lovin' mind." He sat straight and tucked her gun into the front of his pants.

Darby had opportunity. So why didn't she jab her thumb into his side, buck him off her thighs and gain the upper hand? No, she waited for him to threaten her, and God help her, she was curious.

Utterly ridiculous. Where had all her training gone? He didn't *feel* threatening? A total unknown was demanding a package while he *sat* on her. What more did she need to act?

"I can see the wheels turning behind your pretty green eyes." He winced and slid his shirt up to staunch the dark red trickle with the towels.

A waft of blood hit her nostrils. She covered her mouth, trying not to be sick, but her gag reflex kicked in full force.

"God, you're seriously turning sour." He shifted to one side and she scrambled for the bathroom.

She didn't know how long she hurled. Only that after a while, *he* was there, holding her annoying curls away from her face while she grabbed her out-of-control stomach and heaved. She hated her newfound aversion to blood. It was more than embarrassing. If her brothers ever found out, they'd tease her relentlessly.

"You okay now, Officer O'Malley?" he asked, grabbing a washcloth from the top of an unpacked box, wetting it like a nursemaid and handing it to her.

"How do you know who I am?"

"I came looking for you, remember?"

She over-exaggerated her movements to lean against the tub. The porcelain cooled her hot skin. Her visitor might as well think she was still ill instead of capable of ramming her head into his stomach and sending him crashing into the laundry room. If all else failed, she could wait until he really passed out from blood loss or exhaustion.

Which wouldn't be too long from the looks of him.

He swayed, using the doorframe to hold himself upright. Viewed from this angle on the floor, he was especially tall. He continued to hold the dishtowels under his bunched-up shirt with a bloodstained hand.

She gulped down more nausea. "You need a…a doctor."

The stupid jerk had faked getting sick and grinned from ear to ear, leaving her to stare at perfectly aligned teeth. But that was the only thing perfect about his rugged-looking face and two-toned, brown-and-gold hair. A small trail of blood was smeared across his chin from a busted lower lip. His tanned forehead had road rash, with bits of gravel embedded in the lacerations.

This close she could tell his nose had been broken at least once. His strong, square jaw matched that magnificent chest hidden under his loose shirt. The silver dagger dangling around his neck somehow made him as sexy as a pirate instead of creeping her out. And his eyes… Good grief, it looked as if there were a thousand lifetimes in those whiskey-colored spheres.

"What I really need is whatever Pike left for me." He drew a deep breath, grimaced and allowed a short moan to escape. "God, O'Malley, Walter Pike was more than a friend to me. You saw the picture. I'm one of the good guys."

"Who still has my Glock shoved down the front of his pants," she answered, pointing toward her gun.

"Where it's going to stay."

"First things first." She wanted out of the close quarters of the bathroom. "Just how hurt are you?"

"O'Malley." He rolled her name around as if he should be talking with an accent, his eyes never losing contact with hers. "I thought you'd be a bit more, well, manly. Pike never mentioned you were a woman. But we don't have much time."

"I can hold my own. And Pike never gave me anything." It wasn't a lie.

Pike had been shot at the academy and she'd found his body. He managed to say someone would come to her asking for a package, but he died before giving her details. She had no idea what it contained or where it was located. She hated to let her partner down, but she hadn't had any luck finding what Pike had spoken about. Or any luck finding information that would clear her brother of murder charges.

"Right." He sank to the floor, sliding his back down the doorjamb. "Then why was I directed to come here?"

"Let me call an ambulance." Was he acting again or had the adrenaline rush finally worn off?

"No."

"Then your handler."

"No one," he said, fingers on the butt of her gun. "Can't trust…any of them…right now."

Threatening or nonthreatening. She didn't trust herself to choose. For the past several weeks she'd doubted her intuition. Nerves on edge, jumpy, imagining looks from colleagues. And here she was cornered in her bathroom by a thug claiming to work for… Who was he claiming to work for?

"It will complicate my weekend if you die in my hallway." She tried to be detached and uncaring, but this unusual suspect was fading fast. Or was he?

His eyes closed and he coughed—one of those pathetic "ahem" things that didn't convince her one way or the other of his weakening. She inched her way toward the door. Informant or not, she couldn't just wait for him to die.

"I'm undercover DEA." He looked up through pain-filled eyes. She was sunk. "I need your help, O'Malley. Can I depend on you?"

Can I depend on you? The words echoed in her mind.

Two weeks ago, she would have answered yes in a heartbeat. She *had* answered yes—too many times to count. But now no one counted on her. How could they? No one really trusted her. She'd failed Michael, and Pike had died in her arms.

"Verify…two one four…five five five…nine six nine six," he mumbled, fading. "Double-crossed. Don't tell 'em… anything."

RHODES OPENED ONE EYE at a time, wondering why he didn't see swirling stars and birdies. Maybe the tom-toms in his head had scared them all off. Stifling a groan, he inched his way to a sitting position against the door. Every bit of him hurt from his earlier fight, but his side had stopped bleeding and had a bandage.

"Glad to see you're coming around." O'Malley stood in front of him—left hand pointing her department-issued pistol at his head and her right holding a cell phone.

Triumphant and gorgeous. She had to be at least five-nine or five-ten. Slender, with a body honed by the rowing machine in the corner of the living room.

"Who are you and how are you involved with Michael?"

"I already told you, O'Malley."

"Wrong answer." She pushed a button and held the phone to her ear. "Yes, sixteen forty-nine Mayflower Drive. Male, mid-twenties, he's passed out and hit his head. I can't stay on the line, but I'll let them in." She clicked the phone off and sported a very satisfied smile. "You have seven minutes. Tops."

"I'd give us three before the guy sitting on your house busts inside." Another reason he'd used the back entrance. A guy with "cop" written all over him was watching this house from a traditional dark sedan.

"Real answers or you go to the hospital with the cops."

"You *are* the cops, O'Malley."

"Six minutes and counting." She leaned against the bare wall—barely out of his reach, curly hair neatly tucked behind her ear, gun firmly in her hand, sounding confident.

But she was vulnerable. He'd seen her throw up.

"I'm sure it'll be less of a headache to let you become someone else's problem. Not to mention the paperwork that I detest. So convince me."

He needed to be back in control. He inched his way up the doorjamb, his strength steadily returning despite every muscle in his body aching. What was going through her mind? Did she fake the call? Nope, she looked too confident. "I was double-crossed tonight. Hand over the package Pike gave to you, and I'm out of here."

"And the DEA won't help you because…?"

"Can't trust 'em." Okay, raising one very cute eyebrow was her prompt for more information. And the little tug on her Lucky Care Bear T-shirt meant what?

"Why would you think you could trust me?"

Again, the one curious eyebrow thing. Nice. *Don't get distracted, Rhodes.* He was running out of time.

"You saw the photograph. There's only one reason I'd be sent here." That hit a nerve. Her fist tightened around the gun handle. Yeah, she knew about the mysterious package. He could see the indecision playing across her lightly freckled face.

Focus.

"Five minutes," she said in a flat voice, ignoring all the emotion he'd witnessed.

"I'm tracking a guy who might have murdered Pike."

"I'm still listening."

How much could he spill without jeopardizing his next moves? Enough to get them out of here before her shadow parked out front knocked on the door. *Them?* Yes, them. It was the only way he could be sure she told him the truth. And to guarantee no one would be coming after him.

"If the package isn't here, I think we should leave." Someone had her house staked out and Rhodes couldn't tell if the guy in the car would be on her side. "Look. Tonight was supposed to be a simple meet. Get some information. Find out where to go next. I was set up. Trigger-happy cops at one end of the alley and a gun at my back pinning me in the middle. Most likely my handler from the DEA."

"They obviously didn't want you dead or they would have been a little bit more accurate."

"I'm not too sure about that." He pressed his hand to his side. The bleeding had definitely stopped. A flesh wound that still hurt like the devil.

"I can save you a lot of trouble. I didn't set you up and have no information about your…package."

She grinned at the double entendre. Cute.

"Aw, but you do." Yeah, she did. O'Malley wasn't a very good liar. Strange for someone in undercover work. "And you're curious."

"I'll give you that one."

"Shouldn't we be leaving?" They'd be cutting it close by walking out the door now. "Call the number I gave you? Verify my ID."

"Um…cop," she said pointing to herself. "Called it and got the Dallas Celebration Deli while you were unconscious."

"Then I have nothing. Let your curiosity or faith take over. I need your help. You're the only one I can count on."

There it was again. That indecision he'd seen earlier and something more. It would be close if they left right now. Thank God she had a rear-entry garage. "No more delays. They'll be here any minute."

"I'm not turning over whatever Pike left me because you have a map instructing you to come here."

"Take me to the package." He was back in control. He could see how much she wanted to participate. Her eagerness was written all over her face.

Don't say anything else, Rhodes. You'll just screw it up. It has to be her decision.

The whine of an ambulance grew in the distance. He needed to avoid the complication of the Dallas P.D. and deal with the one cop he'd been sent to find—O'Malley. One step and he had his back to her.

Nothing.

A shake of the doorknob.

He knew. Just knew. His thighs tensed, ready to move. His abs hardened, anticipating the requirement of his body.

The front door bashed open and hit the wall. O'Malley turned toward the noise.

There was a pop, a hole in the wall. Someone barely missed shooting a hole in O'Malley's heart.

No time to think, shout or plead. He wrapped one arm around her waist and his free hand around her pistol. He yanked her toward the kitchen, aiming at the target, blindly pulling the trigger.

Chapter Two

Bits of drywall stung Darby's cheek. She landed with a heavy thud on top of the agent who had saved her life. With her snug against his body, his strong arm circled her waist and hauled her into the kitchen. He anchored her to his rock-hard chest, continuing to point her gun at the opening to the hall—his hand wrapped firmly over hers, committing her to action.

The agent's arm pulled so hard and fast, her breath escaped her body. She couldn't move. Or had time slowed to a frame-by-frame? Her eyes blinked. A strand of hair floated across her face, moved by the man behind her.

And still the agent held her locked to his long body. Her legs nesting between his.

Waiting.

A quick intake to fill his lungs. She did the same, but his grip around her middle didn't lessen. No sounds came from the front room. She heard nothing but his matching heartbeat against her back.

"You hit?" Warm air circled her ear, shooting tingles down her spine in spite of their situation.

The still-unnamed agent released his death grip and her hand holding her weapon fell to her leg. She shot to her feet with him quickly following. His eyes locked onto hers while his fingers explored her body.

"Are. You. Hit."

A rough, impatient voice countered the concern in his eyes. Her side was coated in blood—*his* blood. The look she'd seen in his eyes for a split second let her know they had something in common…he'd seen death, too.

"I'm fine." She was anxious to get her eyes back on the crazy SOB who had busted through her door, gun blazing. "Stay here."

Five years of training kicked into gear. Scanning the room and beyond for potential harm, she kept an eye on her unarmed hero. He should have stayed in her kitchen, but he took her flank through the dining room door.

Chest-high bullet holes in her hallway were more than enough evidence that the creep bleeding inside her living room had been shooting to kill. The perp half-sat, half-leaned against her freshly painted—now blood-spattered—wall. Alert. Smug. Shot in the thigh.

"Dallas P.D. Show me your hands." For someone unaccustomed to being shot at, her voice and grip were surprisingly steady. She covered her mystery man as he frisked the shooter. Dealer? Doper? Someone had followed the man who saved her life to her house.

Her DEA agent picked up the weapon several feet from the shooter and slipped it in the back of his jeans. *Her* agent? Definitely not a safe way to think. He had saved her life, but she couldn't completely trust him yet.

The agent had a photo of Pike and the reverse side was a hand-drawn map to her house with doodles around the edges. Doodles to anyone else, but it was a code she and her brothers had used since childhood. The message told her to stick with this man until Michael contacted her. Sent before Michael was shot with Pike's weapon. Sent before he was found comatose on police academy property. She had no reason to trust her brother and even less to trust the outsider carrying the message, but did she have a choice?

"Who wants her dead?" the agent demanded. He smashed the shooter's hands on top of the wound. "You'll want to keep pressure on that."

The shooter sucked air through his teeth in a long hiss.

Blood seemed to be everywhere. But it wasn't. Not this time.

Her hands were covered. No. Her hands were clean.

Swallowing hard did nothing to stop the tremors trying to overtake her body. She took several deep gulps of air, closing her eyes and ignoring the fact that her home was now a crime scene. But closing her eyes didn't keep the image of Pike's death from appearing.

Pike was lying in her arms. Bleeding. Nothing blocked the memory of your partner's life fading away. The tortured look of pain as he struggled to tell her his last secrets would be with her forever.

His screams echoed through the parking lot. Wait, Pike hadn't screamed. Her vision focused on the open mouth of her attacker. His painful roar bounced off the bare walls of her home.

What was the source of his agony? He hadn't been in that much pain when they'd entered the room.

"Tell me." The agent's powerful voice sounded different, more guttural, more vicious. "I only have seconds to find my answers, man. But I can leave you in pain for a long time."

The shooter screamed again when the agent's fist pushed the shooter's hand deeper into the bullet wound. Darby rushed forward. This couldn't be happening. Cops were the good guys.

"Get back." The agent flipped a badge toward her. "He's a cop. A cop who just tried to kill you."

"All right, all right," the shooter yelled. "We're cleaning up loose ends." He hissed through the pain.

The agent didn't stop.

"I swear," the shooter cried. "I was supposed to make it look like a break-in, find the stuff Pike had given her and get rid of the girl."

"We can sort through this train wreck with the correct authorities." Darby should stop him. But she was unwilling to drag the agent from the only person in the room with answers. "There's got to be a logical reason—"

The decision was made for her when the shooter passed out.

"He's a cop. They'll haul us to jail. We won't find our answers while stuck in a holding cell until someone clears this mess up. They might finish what this guy started." He stood and tossed the badge on top of the shooter's chest. "You coming, O'Malley?"

The lights from the ambulance arriving outside flashed through the curtains. Her insides stopped shaking. "We have to call this in."

"Lucky thing that ambulance is out front." He gently turned her around by the shoulders and nudged her toward the kitchen. "We have to go. Now. I'll drive."

He slid past her and swiped her keys from the counter before she could object to anything.

"We can't leave the scene of a shooting."

"We don't have time for a discussion. The EMTs are here." He yanked on her right arm, keeping her from returning to the front of the house. "That dirtbag tried to kill us. He admitted they're after Pike's package."

"I've got this man," the first EMT shouted, coming through the doorway. "This is a badge. Call dispatch, officer down."

It took a second to register the vise grip around her upper arm. And yet another second for her to accept how much trouble she'd be in once she left her house.

Oh yeah, she was leaving.

Following her brother's instructions to stick with the agent might possibly clear Michael from suspicion and find Pike's real murderer. She'd keep her word to her dead partner and save her brother.

"O'Malley, we have to go. Now."

"Right after you hand over the shooter's weapon."

Secret Agent Man released her arm, pulled the .38 from the middle of his back and handed it to her. No argument, but he slammed through the door. She scooped up her gun belt, running close behind. He punched the opener button and ran to the driver's side.

With their doors barely closed, he revved the engine and tore out of the alley. He zigzagged through the streets until he reached Central Expressway.

She squirmed enough in her seat to watch in case someone followed. She'd halfway expected to be in cuffs by this point, not in the clear. She stowed the shooter's weapon in the compartment between the seats and holstered her gun, keeping it in her lap in case her companion did something crazy.

"North or south?"

"South." Toward her office. Toward the familiar. Toward safety.

"South it is," he said casually, driving like a law-abiding citizen, turning onto the highway as if nothing were wrong. "You should remove the battery from your phone."

He was right again. She had a data phone with GPS capability that the police could track. The lights from Central Expressway illuminated the dismantling process that left her disconnected from anyone familiar.

"Why did that man follow you to my house and try to kill you?" she asked five minutes down the road.

"Didn't he say he was after *you,* Officer O'Malley?"

"Let's cut the cutesy crap, shall we? Pull over at an all-night gas station. I need a minute to process what happened." Maybe she should wave her gun to emphasize she was in charge. "And it's Detective."

Or it used to be before she'd been transferred to the academy.

"So we'll need gas?" he asked, avoiding yet another question and darting his eyes to the rearview mirror.

"Look. I still don't know who you are and Pike wasn't all that clear about who the package was for. He didn't mention anyone by name."

"And you didn't open it?" He smiled a toothy grin in her direction. "You strike me as the curious type."

He was confident and arrogant about his decisions. He'd done this before. Run. Evade the police. Shoot suspects or worse. Some of his experience was beginning to piss her off. Most she was beginning to admire.

"Don't pretend to know me. We're only twenty minutes from where I report for duty. So cool it."

He lifted his fingers off the steering wheel in mock surrender. The next exit approached and he crossed three lanes of traffic to come to a screeching halt on the shoulder.

"What the heck are you doing?" she yelled.

"Keep your eyes open, O'Malley. Good surveillance requires more than one person. I'm looking for a second car."

Automatically turning in her seat, she watched as four cars sped past.

"You don't seriously believe that man was a cop?"

"Don't you? His badge looked authentic to me." He swiveled in his seat to face her instead of the mirror he'd been staring at. "Pike sent for *me*. In my book, that means he couldn't trust anyone near him. Bad guys. Bad cops." He shrugged. "Doesn't make any difference to me. Somebody killed Pike and I'll return the favor."

"Pike meant a lot to me, too." But so did Michael. She wouldn't let this mystery agent find anything without her.

Not when the most obvious path to Pike's killer might lead him to her brother. She needed to be certain he avoided that particular road. "What could be so important that Pike would be killed before anyone even knows what it is? Why would cops want to make this mysterious thing disappear along with anyone who knows about it?"

"I promised to deliver it to the DEA. I'll let them sort out all the whys. Don't worry about my end. Just take me to it."

"I prefer to drive." She removed the keys and shot out the door, walking around the tail of the car while he circled the hood.

What was she doing? Was this DEA bad boy truly Pike's friend or someone wanting the package to destroy it? She'd find whatever Pike had hidden and the truth. Cops trying to kill her didn't make sense, but neither did this agent. Quick on the draw, saving her life—she understood that was part of the job. But even her own father had never held her hair while she'd thrown up.

Was she totally out of her mind? Shoot, she already knew the answer. She'd fled the scene of a crime. A man—a cop— had been shot with her duty weapon. And her job was history. Her only ray of hope was if this guy was legitimate. They could explain what happened to his supervisor, retrace Pike's steps and find the missing pieces. It was her best, perhaps her only, chance of helping her brother, getting justice for her old mentor and hanging on to whatever shred of what might be her career.

If the agent could connect the dots to prove Michael's in- nocence, she'd lend him the pencil.

"Let's start with something simple…your name." She shoved her weapon into the door pocket, unsnapping the se- curity strap of the holster. Easy access if something went wrong.

"Now that we'll be working together I guess you should know. Erren Rhodes to your rescue."

"I'm not working with you."

"Isn't it a little too late for that decision?" He turned in the seat, leaning back toward the door window. "Look. All we need to do is retrieve Pike's package and you're done. Back to whatever boring job you do."

Boring was correct. She wanted out in the field. More specifically, she wanted to be undercover. She'd spent years analyzing other officers' work, verifying accounts of operations and preparing case information. She'd longed to be in the field. Instead she'd been transferred to the academy.

Whoever this man was, he was her clue to unraveling this mystery and she would stick with him to find her answers. It had to be the cop in her telling her she could handle this guy. After all, she had the gun, right?

Right. That's why a voice in her head kept screaming she must be completely and utterly nuts. It would be easier if it were the Sergeant Major's voice droning in her ear about making the wrong decision. Truth was, she hadn't heard her father's voice in a long time. Nope, it was *her* voice asking questions.

"This'll take some getting used to," he said. "I've never worked with anyone before. You're in, O'Malley. Admit it."

"So how do we avoid every cop in the city who will be searching for us?" Every instinct told her that trusting this man would help clear her brother's name.

"You mean they'll be searching for *you*," he stated, very certain of himself. "They don't know who I am yet."

"Someone knows you're in Dallas. Didn't you say they ambushed you?"

"You're probably right." His nod was a silhouette against the passing cars. "Start by taking me to the package. We'll open it up and find out what we're dealing with."

"This is ridiculous, Agent Rhodes."

"Cut the agent bit. It's too easy to slip up in front of the wrong person. Call me Erren or honey or babe."

She watched him fix that gorgeous smile back on his face. Yes, it was totally for her benefit. And it was halfway doing its job.

"It doesn't matter. I won't be approved to work with you."

"Who are we asking?"

Erren stared as O'Malley didn't crack a smile.

"You aren't sanctioned for this operation?" She continued to nervously drum her fingers on the console between the seats. "There's no chance your supervisor can help clear this incident? No safe contact?"

"Let's say the DEA will be ecstatic when I'm not causing any more problems. Pike was my safe contact. Always has been."

"Good grief, you can't mean to find Pike's killer completely on your own. Especially with no plan or backup or resources."

"I've got you, babe."

"Why do you need me?"

Erren had no specific answer, but wasn't it obvious? She wasn't his partner, only an unanswered question in his investigation.

"Somehow Pike's death has connected us, O'Malley."

"Do you have a theory about *that?*"

"I don't know who left the map leading me to your house." Had she opened her eyes the slightest bit wider? "Maybe *you* do. Can we discuss this while you drive?"

Glowering, his reluctant detective turned the key, shoved her Camry in gear and merged back into traffic. The photo had come from Butthead. His working theory? Beavis and Butthead would pick him up, follow the map and kill them both in her living room, leaving the picture. He didn't know why yet…it was only a theory.

But something more than Pike's picture had convinced her to come with him. He didn't care why as long as she delivered Pike's stuff and he could finish the job. He would find the murderer, give him what he deserved and disappear. Simple. Yeah, he definitely had a plan.

"Tell me exactly what's going on."

"I was ambushed. My cover's blown. And my Dallas handler disappeared when shots were fired."

"If they decided to take you out, no offense, but it wouldn't require an ambush or shooting their own men. And that doesn't explain the Dallas P.D.'s involvement."

That x-ray vision of hers was starting to unnerve him. She looked as if she could see through the persona he cloaked himself with on the street. The same personality that had kept him alive for six years. He couldn't afford to exchange innuendos or smiles with her, just the facts.

"It was a setup. Whoever was at the end of the alley wasn't with Beavis and Butthead. Those two guys were as surprised to see the cops as I was."

"Or impersonators," she said loyally. She wasn't naïve, just staunch. Even after a dirty cop tried to kill her.

"I tried to surrender, but they kept firing."

"And missed." There she went shaking her head again. "So what were they really after? Your credibility? What's your usual procedure when something like this happens?"

"Never happened."

Why did he suddenly *sound* as if he was lying? He was an excellent liar. But he was telling the truth. So why did her questioning make him feel like a liar? He must have hit his head harder than he remembered. "I have to be close to something, because they want me out of the picture. But why not dead?"

"Dead doesn't go away." Her voice was emotionless and unsettling. "It gets cops crawling out of the woodwork, which is something they probably don't need."

Right answer. And logical. Pike had said O'Malley was one of the best. Yeah, she might have that rare quality he could admire. And admiration wasn't something he spared for too many people—especially cops. Strangely, it was there the first time he'd looked into the detective's emerald-green eyes. And he still didn't know her first name.

"If I help you—"

"If?" Better for her to know there wasn't a choice.

She shot him a look like… Just what was that look? Cute, yes. That one curious eyebrow thing suggested *he* was the crazy one and she was totally in control.

"If I decide to help you, we're partners," she stated.

"Now wait a minute."

"Equal in all decisions."

"I don't care how much undercover experience you think you have."

"Equals." Looking straight ahead, she was confident again and his insides were jumping.

"Nope." He didn't really have a choice and he could see the control slipping from his fingers. What was it about this woman that got under his skin? "No way."

Lie.

All he had to do was lie. Agree with her until he got the package. Other than "south," she'd given no other directions. He still didn't have a clue where they were headed. He could lead her to believe they were collaborating. Nothing new about that. So why did he feel compelled to be honest?

"This is for real, O'Malley. Don't think for a second they won't kill us." Even in the dark, he was certain her knuckles turned white from her death grip on the wheel. "We can pretend to be equals, but it'll be my experience that's going to keep us alive. Got it?"

Truth had spewed from his mouth. She must have agreed since she didn't disagree. He leaned back in the seat, very aware of the condition of his clothes. Everything hurt. His side wasn't exactly on fire, but it wasn't nice and comfy either. He clamped his hand over the wet gauze. As long as he stayed immobile he was fine, but he needed a couple of stitches or some Krazy Glue.

"I guess you should issue your orders using my name. It's Darby."

The unusual name fit. Darby O'Malley. Nice. A complete Irish bundle with dazzling red hair.

"Can you make out that alert sign?" she asked.

They were on a major thoroughfare cutting through Dallas, and the flashing alert ahead of them had nothing to do with road construction.

"Abducted. White female. Suspect armed. Silver Camry TX SGT MJR3." It was worse than he'd originally thought, but he couldn't let O'Malley know that. "You have personalized plates?"

"How can they think I was abducted? He said he was a cop."

"The cop lied. You're a smart woman. Don't you know how the real world works?"

"What could he accomplish? He shot up my house and nearly killed us."

"Darby." She wasn't going to like what he was about to say. "He'll report I had your weapon and fired first. The entire state will be looking for this car and the man who abducted a cop. I've shot another. It's the perfect excuse to fire first and ask questions later. And you'll probably be hit in the cross fire."

"You don't have any proof. He didn't even know you were there."

Her loyalty would be their downfall. He could predict that scenario easily enough. She trusted law enforcement too completely.

"I spotted the cop watching you on the first pass by your house. He probably got notification of your 911 call featuring an injured white male."

"I knew he was after you."

"Wrong. They're after whatever Pike left in your care. Remember?" It wasn't hard to notice her sharp, indrawn breath and the quirk of her eyebrow. "You asked about your brother earlier. Is there another reason the cops are interested?"

"Michael's wanted for questioning."

Her hesitation gave her away. She was lying. He could figure out why later. Right now he had to keep them free from any authority who would prevent him from working the case. He wasn't quitting until he had proof enough to put a needle in the arm of Pike's murderer.

She changed lanes quickly, heading for an exit.

"Stay on the highway. It might be better to take a side road, but we'll be in Mesquite in fifteen minutes. There's a gas station that sells T-shirts off Interstate 30. I don't think we should try to pick anything up in this car."

She didn't object. She didn't talk for several minutes.

"There's no one you can call to let them know what we're doing?" she eventually asked, her voice seeking the confirmation they were proceeding down the correct path.

"I don't trust anybody. Neither should you."

He heard her low throaty growl of frustration. He closed his eyes again, trying to recall the handler's face who had set him up so thoroughly tonight.

Strangely enough he could only picture Darby at the moment she chose to help him. The panic that flooded her eyes had been conquered and set aside with one determined heartbeat.

This woman was more than under his skin and he hadn't even known her a full hour.

Chapter Three

"Cuffs?" Erren asked. "Do we really need to go there?"

Darby killed the engine and twisted between the steering wheel and the backseat where she'd thrown the bulky gun belt earlier.

"On the off chance you're thinking you don't need me to retrieve Pike's package, think again. You're also a suspect in a shooting and not going anywhere without me."

"Just for the record." There was an abundance of self-confidence in his every action. Even while he leaned from the passenger seat to snap the cuffs into place—one around each wrist with the steering wheel between. "This is the last time we'll need to do this."

"Really?"

"I'll be giving the orders if you want to tag along to find Pike's murderer." God, he reeked of arrogance. "I can do this op in my sleep."

The man was a complete conundrum. Smiling one minute, burnt-out agent the next. She popped the trunk and went for her jacket, slipping her Glock into the pocket.

Covering her blood-soaked T-shirt, she retrieved the keys from the seat, slammed the door and trotted to the restroom to clean up. She yanked the shirt from her body and shoved it deep into the trash can, splashing cold water on her flushed skin. Wetting paper towels, she smeared the blood on her side to a weak pink stain. The smear would have to do. She shook the drops of water from her fingers and zipped her jacket to the neck.

She'd taken four minutes. Tops. But the sinking feeling in her stomach bubbled into her throat as she opened the restroom door and looked out the glass storefront.

Her car was gone.

"I am such an idiot!" She ran out and around the corner, finding no trace of her vehicle.

"I wouldn't say that, Detective."

Heaven help her, he'd gotten close enough that his breath warmed her neck. Tingles traveled to every nerve ending in her body. Her hand jumped to her pocket. Empty.

"Looking for this?"

Darby fisted her fingers, spun around and knocked the agent's hands in the air. Instead of dislodging the gun, he avoided the collision, ejected the magazine and the round from the chamber. In a mere couple of seconds, he was holding her weapon on his palm, stretching it toward her.

"Holy cow. Take it easy. If I'd wanted a gun, I would have taken the one from the console."

She snatched the pistol back a split second later. But not before her cold fingers had been pierced by his warmth.

"How—"

"Master pickpocket, a handy talent I acquired my first year undercover. Also helps getting rid of the bracelets." He shook his left wrist where the handcuffs were still attached. "I removed the ignition key from your ring while you were getting your jacket."

Rookie move. She hadn't left the keys in the seat—he had. She shoved the gun back into her jacket. The last thing they needed was for some overanxious gas clerk to call in a robbery.

"Who *are* you?" This guy was good and she *was* a complete idiot. But it wouldn't happen again.

Erren raised a finger, pointed toward the car parked in the dark along the back fence. "No one's going to ding it there. And they might not notice those custom plates if we're lucky."

If she spoke, she'd sputter. She was certain of it and very grateful he saved her from responding when he headed inside the convenience store. She followed. No one else was around, but she wasn't taking any more risks. She stood at the men's door, hearing him curse the man who had hit his face. While the air blower rumbled to life and echoed off the restroom tile, she paid for a notepad and two Texas souvenir T-shirts.

Why deny that the man was good at what he did?

She shook her shoulders, attempting to free herself from the tingle still within her body. If she had any sense, she'd have the clerk call 911. Let the real police sort through the mess. Proper channels, that's what she needed. Not a chance. "Going rogue" with her mysterious and most certainly dangerous new partner was exactly the choice she needed. She could tell herself it was for Pike and Michael, but the quiver that went through her body... The reaction when his breath had skittered along her neck made her wonder if those were her only reasons.

No matter what, she couldn't allow his mysterious appeal to derail her from her mission—proving Michael's innocence.

He opened the door and her brain stalled. His hair was slicked back and a richer dark brown. No two-tone golds in sight. She tossed the shirt, hitting his bare chest. Standing in the open doorway, he pulled the red, white and blue cotton over his head and across the best abs she'd ever seen.

"I'll wait outside."

The T-shirt hugged the abs she had to stop thinking about. She didn't wait. He followed right on her heels.

"Don't feel bad, sweetheart." His arm brushed hers as they rounded the corner.

"Who said I did?" Had he caught her ogling him?

"You. Every emotion you have is plainly displayed for the average Joe to see." A small speck of blood on his forehead indicated he'd dug the gravel from his scrape. "It'll be better if you stick to the truth as much as possible. Or don't say anything."

"What are you talking about?"

He kept his hand against his side with those long legs of his moving at a steady pace toward the car. No one would have guessed he'd been knifed.

She tossed the plastic sack in the backseat. Shoot. The cocky SOB had gotten her out of the store before she'd put the shirt on. She couldn't leave him alone again. The jacket would have to do.

It was preposterous to think she was running from the police. Paranoid to think a cop tried to kill them. Unbelievable to think she felt safer in her car with a stranger than at home. And totally logical that she'd do anything to find her brother and clear his name.

The door shut, rocking the car ever so slightly. Unlike her self-confidence, which was rocked to her core.

"Well, Darby, where to now?"

"We need another car. My brother won't ask any questions." But the Sergeant Major certainly would.

"I thought you said your brother was missing."

"My younger brother, Michael. Yes." She put the car in gear and pulled away. "My older brother Sean is in Plano this weekend."

"Will we be asking for his vehicle or exchanging?"

There was enough surrounding light to distinguish that hint of conceit and rogue smile.

Dear God, it was too embarrassing to think she was

attracted to this DEA agent. But why not? His dry wit hadn't turned disrespectful with her inexperience. She would concentrate on what she did best. Attraction didn't help but it wouldn't hinder them finding her brother.

"ERREN. COME ON, WAKE UP."

Darby's sensual voice penetrated a fog in Erren's brain, a depth he rarely allowed himself to get to while on a job. A real dream. And he had a weird feeling Darby had been the star. He inched his lids open. The sun ricocheted off the mirror straight into his eyes.

"I fell asleep?"

Darby leaned on the steering wheel, furiously writing. The details of her face were hidden by her crazy, curly hair falling in front of a rounded cheekbone.

"Understatement. You've been snoring like an asthmatic hound for a couple of hours."

Him? Sleep? Not possible. He'd blame it on the knife wound and call it passing out. Twice in one night? Never happened. He'd never live it down. Of course, no one would ever know. Darby had no one to tell, and he couldn't joke about it with Pike.

Pike was permanently gone.

Shifting so the warmth of the sun left his face, he flexed his stiff muscles. Stretched his side. No pain.

Darby paused, placing the tip of the pen in her mouth and tapping it between her teeth. That type of annoying habit usually bothered him, but he was more concerned with the intense concentration in her eyes when she faced him.

"Time to go. They're almost up," she said matter-of-factly, but placed the pen back to her paper, continuing to write.

This brother must be an early riser. Most days about this time, Erren was heading to bed. He hid a yawn behind a full stretch of his arms. He'd live on a couple of hours of sleep. But what about his new partner?

The pen stopped racing back and forth in her fingers. She tapped it a couple of times against the steering wheel, then wrote something on the paper and closed the notebook. She'd made some type of decision the previous night. Something had convinced her to stay with him. Whether it was searching for the package or finding out why the cops wanted her out of the way—it didn't matter.

Taking credit would be nice, but realistically, she couldn't trust him this soon. Whatever had happened to keep her on his side, he liked this confident woman.

"Anywhere to get coffee around here?" he asked, catching his first look at where they were. "Somewhere in this field? I thought we were heading to your brother's place."

They were parked next to a truck connected to a small trailer. He couldn't see around it, blocked by yet another truck on the far side. Trees stood in front of them and cars lined the road to their left. There seemed to be a lot of empty cars, but no people.

"We're parked next to my brother's truck. I'm sure the Sergeant Major's got a thermos of coffee at his camp." She looked at her watch. "But we won't be here that long." She placed the notepad in the console and turned the key to lock it away. "Tic Tac?"

He held out his hand and she shook two of the breath mints from their container. "Okay, I'm as curious as the next guy. What were you writing? And who is the Sergeant Major?"

"It's a summary of last night. I'm documenting our movements. Things tend to get jumbled together if an officer waits too long to write down his or her notes."

Cops like her made cops like him nervous. He'd have to get a look later on. First things first. They needed another vehicle.

"Time to move. The balloon's up and the Sergeant Major will be headed to the john." She got out of the car and he followed around the parked trucks into a crowd of people.

"Balloon? And who is this Sergeant Major?" What the Sam Hill was she leading him into? A brother is one thing, but a sergeant major of what exactly?

"Yeah, it's the Plano Balloon Festival."

"And your brother is working here?" His confidence slipped a notch with the nervousness he recognized in his voice. Things lifting off the ground always made him edgy.

"They're amateur balloonists. He and my dad own their own rig. It's the *Young Blades* balloon."

Did she know she was talking in code?

They wove in and out of busy people, half-inflated balloons and giant baskets lying on their sides. No one questioned them and a few people even waved at Darby. It was obvious that she was at home and in her element.

"You might want to keep your head down. Someone might have heard about your disappearance," he advised.

"It's not much farther." She ignored his advice and waved at another couple.

Erren watched her stride through the bedlam. Clearly these people were crazy to inflate objects to carry them where only birds were meant to go. Hot air balloons ranked just below hang gliding and parasailing. Skydiving would never be on the list since he'd never be in an airplane.

Give him a knife fight in a dark alley any day.

"Sean's not alone yet." She came to an abrupt halt. "Hold on."

Turning her back on an inflated balloon and the two men securing ropes, she brushed off imaginary lint from his shoulders. Definitely hiding her face from the men.

The balloon was huge, dwarfing the trees, with markings like gold blades or sabers against an array of army drab.

"I think the guy you keep referring to as the Sergeant Major headed south."

She peeked over her shoulder, spun and almost skipped to her brother. Same build, same hair, same features. It looked better on Darby.

"Hey, Sean."

"Cool, I didn't think you could make it this weekend." Sean finished securing the balloon. "The Sergeant Major's in for a surprise."

"More than you know." Darby gave the man about his age a hug.

"Who's this?" Sean jerked his head toward Erren.

"Richard Paladin. Nice to meet you." He stuck his hand out, received a solid shake and a complete once-over from big brother.

Darby's eyebrow shot straight up, but she also gave him an approving look for using a different name.

"What's up? Why didn't you call?"

Erren turned to give her a bit of privacy, and took the opportunity to look around. No Sergeant Major guy in sight. No police cars that he could see. Nothing to indicate they would be spotted and hauled to jail for attempted kidnapping or murder.

The siblings whispered, but weren't completely quiet.

"He'll never go for it," Sean exploded, his voice loud and sharp. He backed away from Darby. "I won't let you ruin your career for Michael. He's in a coma, guarded in a hospital somewhere. We can't be there for him anymore. You have to stop."

"He's innocent," she said.

So Michael was her true motivation? Good to know.

"Let the police prove it. When are you going to admit that he's not one of the good guys?"

"I have to do this, Sean. He'd do it for us. You know he

would." But her voice wasn't laced with complete conviction. "All I need is your truck."

"I don't loan my truck to anyone."

"Keys, please."

Darby held out her hand and her brother dug in his pocket, pulling out keys. The words being spoken didn't reflect their actions, but he couldn't relate. He hadn't experienced this type of relationship. No brothers or sisters and no family since high school. If they weren't in a hurry, he'd want to examine their actions more.

"Anything else?"

"Well, if you could let the Sergeant Major know I'm working undercover and haven't been abducted."

"Is that all?" Sean scrubbed his face with both hands, clearly exasperated.

"Time to go, Darby. Cop at ten o'clock." Erren placed himself between Darby and the Sergeant Major, who was headed their way with a police officer.

"If they find you here, you won't make it past the perimeter gate," Sean warned.

Darby looked at Erren. "Quick. Into the basket."

"We can't hide in a basket." Was she crazy? He wasn't getting in that death trap. Not even to escape. His gut tightened, tying knots on top of the knots already there.

"We'll go up," Darby insisted. "Tell him Richard's proposing."

"You know he'll never—"

"We'll already be in the air. Tell him the guy paid you five hundred."

Sean shook his head. "He's going to be megapissed."

Erren heard the conversation, but it didn't register. The cop was closing in and the thought of going up had his blood pounding in his ears. "Nothing short of a gun to my head will make me get in that thing."

"How about cuffs around your wrists? And this time, they won't be mine."

"Not happening." He searched the crowd for another option.

"We've spent all night avoiding the police because you believed there's a conspiracy. If we're going to retrieve Pike's package, we have to be free of the authorities." With an exasperated huff, she grabbed his arm and tugged him forward. "Get in the basket. Now."

She was right. The cop advanced. There was one way out. Up.

He hated...up.

"I've got it, Sean. Thanks. This should work."

There wasn't a step, so he hopped over the side, trying not to think about the consequences.

"Yeah, but you'll have to deal with the Sergeant Major when you come down," her brother said.

"I know." Darby's voice was softer, less authoritative than when she'd ordered him into the balloon.

Erren stayed on the floor of the basket. Maybe if he couldn't see the dang thing floating in the air, he wouldn't lose yesterday's lunch. Maybe he wouldn't shake right out of his shoes. Maybe. Just maybe.

Concentrate on the weave of the wicker. It was only a bigger version of the baskets his grandmother made. He could do this. They couldn't get caught. It was the only way to avoid days of sorting out the truth or being thrown off the case entirely. Nothing to it.

Maybe.

Darby climbed in, opened a valve and the smell of propane filled the air. She immediately used a striker to spark a flame. The swoosh of the gas springing to life shot through him with an image of the stupid air sack going up in flames like the *Hindenburg*.

The balloon rose and Erren kept his butt firmly glued to the bottom of the basket.

"What are you doing down there? You need to stand up. It's a real clear morning. You can see for several miles. Besides, you're supposed to be proposing."

"Proposing?" He tilted his head and watched the wind whip her hair from her face. She really was lovely. "Why would I be proposing?"

"You really weren't paying attention, were you?" She quirked an eyebrow at him before returning her attention to the heater. "It's the only reason the Sergeant Major lets the balloon go up without him. He can't stand the mushy stuff."

"Got it." There was no way in hell he was standing up. "But I'm not the type of guy to go down on one knee."

"Are you at least the kind who can stand up? It's hard to sell a proposal if the Sergeant Major can't see you do it."

"Not really, Darby."

"Are you kidding me? What's wrong with you?" Her forehead scrunched up with her questions. "You're as white as a sheet."

"No descriptions necessary. I'm—"

"They're here," she whispered strongly. "Stand up."

"Can't do it."

"This has happened before?"

"Every time." Every rooftop. Every tree climbed on a dare. "As long as I can't see where I am, I can still imagine we're on the ground." The basket swung back and forth like a swing. His body flinched, totally beyond his control. "Except when that happens."

"Where's the big Secret Agent Man saving my life when I need him?"

Not in this death trap.

"The Sergeant Major will bring us down immediately if he

thinks something's wrong. Sorry, tough guy, pull it together. Stand up."

Her hands were under his arms, tugging, before he could fight it. So he was the *big Secret Agent Man?* He could play that role. Right? Just another cover. He inched his way to a standing position. His chest tightened to a not-breathing level. The basket swayed a little, but seemed steady enough. They were still tethered to the ground by ropes. He'd seen them before hopping inside.

"So what do couples do up here when the guy proposes?" His hands shook against the basket's leather rail. His abdomen clenched, giving him more than his normal workout.

"They definitely look more excited than you do at the moment." She took a step closer to him. The basket swayed more. "Erren, look at me."

He did. Straight into dark green pools sparkling in the morning sun. It was easy to concentrate on them. To see nothing else as they grew closer and blocked out the treetops serving as their backdrop.

"Don't freak out," she whispered, dusting the top of his shoulders with her fingers. Letting her hands linger on his upper arms wasn't his choice, but definitely kept her close enough so he couldn't see his surroundings.

She drew closer and closer. Each second was imprinted in his mind like a frame of a film. Her actions ticked away like a silent movie. Then her lips touched his. Nature conquered fear.

His hands were on her slim, firm waist instead of the cool leather trimming the top of the basket. He couldn't close his eyes completely. He watched her reaction, felt her body relax. She anchored them to the center brace in the basket, but arched her body toward him.

He'd wanted to kiss her since first straddling her strong body the night before. His fingers inched up under the windbreaker to feel bare skin. No shirt. Interesting. They inched farther, exploring her cool silk, feeling her jump slightly, feeling her body move into his, feeling one of her hands flutter up his back.

God, her lips were smooth and ideal. Her mouth was warm. A perfect fit. Everything was a perfect fit. They weren't coming up for air. The kiss kept deepening. Her breasts pressed into his chest. He couldn't wait to get his hands on them and find out if they were a perfect fit, too.

"Hey, d'Artagnan," Sean shouted from below. "Come on down."

Darby drew back, leaving inches between them. Her finger caressed the outline of his ear, trailing down his neck and tapped the dagger charm hanging there.

"You can sit now." Did he imagine the huskiness in her voice? She broke away from his arms. "I need to open the parachute valve so we'll descend."

Tops of balloons were to his left and nothing but air to his right. Tree tops were in the distance across the field as he stumbled back to the edge of the basket.

His legs shook and his insides jumped, but was it from the height? Or a green-eyed witch who had taken him flying?

Chapter Four

"Time to face the firing squad."

Darby muttered under her breath, but Agent Rhodes shifted, letting her know he'd heard the sibling battle cry for facing their father.

Agent Rhodes… Or should she think of him as Erren after that erotic kiss? She hadn't meant the distraction to go so far. A little shock therapy to take his mind off his obvious fear of heights. And judging by the raised voices below, everyone had seen her complete enjoyment of his marvelous kissing ability.

Unfortunately, her head was coming down out of the clouds rather quickly and her feet were about to hit the ground.

"I can hear the Sergeant Major yelling at Sean for letting the balloon go up."

"Are you going to tell me who this Sergeant Major guy is?"

Erren was still standing. A little rocky on his feet, but he looked much better than when she'd thought he was about to hurl. He made eye contact with her for the first time since their kiss. Whew, what a kiss. The man had a way to focus and bring concentrated effort to the task at hand. He'd been the one who could barely stand. But when *her* knees got a smidgen shaky, it was his arm steadying her, feeling its way around her waist, discovering there wasn't a shirt under the jacket. Her body had quickly grown hot enough to keep the balloon in the air without propane, but taking anything off wasn't an option….

"Does your brother work for him?" Erren asked.

It was probably time to break the bad news. "Sergeant Major is short for father. Three boys and one girl and we all refer to him as the Sergeant Major. Even though he's retired, he's still U.S. Army through and through."

"And you call him Sergeant Major?" he asked, with his eyes closed. Still unable to watch their surroundings.

"You'll know why in a few minutes." Couldn't he hear the yelling from directly below them? A controlled, raised voice. Nothing so loud the festival participants could hear, but a loud voice nonetheless. She couldn't hear Sean's responses yet, but they were almost to the ground. "You better let me do the talking when we land. My father doesn't deal well with a change in his plans."

"I can handle it."

Erren looked steadier on his feet. The green hint of nausea was quickly being replaced by a shoulders-back, ramrod-spine, no-frills kind of guy. If she didn't know any better, she would think Erren had exited the cabin of a military jet.

"Got a rubber band or something?" He tugged at his hair, shoving the longish locks behind his ears.

"Nothing." She patted her pockets to make certain.

"You did not say your sister was in the basket. She's the one getting engaged?" The Sergeant Major's voice boomed from beneath them.

"Not for real, sir." Sean explained while gathering the ropes. "I couldn't let the cops take her in. Hear her out."

"Cops? Why would they— She *is* a cop."

The ground rapidly approached. Erren ripped a piece of his T-shirt and tied his hair at the back of his neck. He shoved the red, white and blue Don't Mess with Texas shirt into his pants and pulled them higher on his waist, tightening his belt.

"Get ready for a bump," she instructed, attempting to ignore the discussion below, praying her father wasn't drawing a crowd and watching Erren change personas right before her eyes.

Gone was the man too afraid to stand up in the basket. He'd been replaced by a man her father would have a hard time finding fault with. Well, except for the small necklace dangling against his tanned neck. And maybe the very intimate, public kiss.

"You might want to put your dagger in your pocket."

The basket touched ground, ropes were tied, they hopped over the side and the chain and charm were gone.

"What's the big idea stealing my balloon to avoid questioning, young woman?" Her father didn't touch her. He had completely dispensed with pleasantries or introductions and gone straight for the jugular...as usual. "I have no use for men who show their affections in public, son. You're dismissed while I speak with my daughter."

"Begging the Sergeant Major's pardon, but I'm the person your daughter was protecting with that kiss. I believe it's in your best interest to hear me out."

"And who the heck are you?"

A very good question and one she was curious about herself.

"Paladin, sir."

Her father's lip lifted, almost growing to a smile before he caught the reaction and put his Sergeant Major face back in place. What was she missing?

Her father actually clapped a hand on a stranger's shoulder and led him to his coffee thermos.

"Spit it out, son. What's your story?"

Erren nodded his head but they were too far away for her to hear his words.

"Are you seeing what I'm seeing?" her brother whispered behind her, holding her in place.

She twisted away from watching the clap on Erren's shoulder to face an awestruck brother, mesmerized by the scene.

"If you're witnessing our father miss the opportunity to flail me alive for messing with his—"

"Our."

"*The* balloon," she corrected. "Then yes, I guess we're not hallucinating."

She took a step to follow Erren, but Sean tugged on her elbow. She didn't want her father involved and had no idea what Erren might tell him.

"Darb'tagnan."

She loved the childhood nickname her siblings had given her. The O'Malley brothers had all been the Three Musketeers growing up and one day to join their fun antics, she'd declared herself d'Artagnan. The name had morphed into "Darb'tagnan" and her siblings had developed "four-teer," a secret language of drawings to bypass random babysitters or adults.

"Let *Paladin* the chameleon handle the Sergeant Major." He waved for her to follow him to the other side of the basket. "What happened to him up there? He did an about-face on the scared-spitless routine. Which is the real him?"

"That's the thing, Sean. This guy was sent by Pike and—"

"Your partner at the academy? Not to be tactless, but how can you believe him? Isn't he a little late?"

How much should she tell him? "He had a note from Michael, telling me in four-teer language to stick with him."

"And that's enough to make you run to Michael's rescue again? You're determined to believe him? Didn't his academy embarrassment teach you anything? Or him breaking into your old apartment?" He pushed his hands through his hair, his level of frustration apparent. "God, Darb, our little brother is headed down a path we can't go. I agree with the Sergeant Major—it's best to just wait for him to hit rock bottom and straighten himself out."

"Don't you think lying in a coma and being an accused cop killer is rock bottom enough? He can't defend himself."

"Maybe you're right. I give up." He stuck his hands into his pockets. "You're going through with this? No way to talk you out of it?" He had one of those big-brother faces on—the kind he gave her when he was in charge after Connor had left for boot camp.

"I have to find out the truth."

"That's what I was afraid of." He took her hand and closed her fingers around a wad of cash. "You're going to need more. This is all I have on me."

"I'll pay you back."

She didn't argue since she did need the money. She only had a twenty in her purse after buying the T-shirts. "Thanks."

"Thank me by staying safe and out of jail, will ya?" He gave her a quick hug. "You're a good cop, sis, and if you need to find out what Michael was doing or how he's involved…do it."

"I will prove he's innocent."

"That's what I don't get, Darby. Michael *admitted* he's guilty and you still believe in his innocence. We're all horrible liars, you know that."

"I'll stay in touch, but not with my phone. I'm taking Richard to Pike's house to have a look around and see what I can find."

Her brother nodded toward their father, who still had a hand on Erren's shoulder, still nodding, not yelling. Strange behavior.

"Whoever that fellow with the Sergeant Major is, he's good. Real good. Don't trust him and don't…" He arched his eyebrows and gave her a birds-and-bees kind of nod. "You know."

Even though Sean didn't say the words, she didn't miss his look of "don't sleep with him." It would be unethical to sleep with her partner, no matter how incredible of a kisser he happened to be.

"What happened to your face, son?"

"Job hazard, sir." With the exception of last night and perhaps once or twice in San Antonio, he hadn't been in too many fights. Although he trained most of the time. This one had left him a little ragged looking. The others had broken his nose. Twice.

"Being roughed up didn't seem to stop my daughter in the balloon."

"My apologies, Sergeant Major." But he wouldn't be apologizing to Darby. After this operation was over, he'd be revisiting that scene…if she were open to the idea.

"Paladin is a character from *Have Gun—Will Travel,* an old television show from the early sixties I used to watch. My name is Denny O'Malley, U.S. Army sergeant major retired, and where I come from, a man gives his real name and rank. So who the hell are you?"

He needed some type of connection or cooperation from the Sergeant Major without blowing his cover. It would help to avoid the police, but the people who were after Darby might come after her family. Leaving them blind wasn't a risk he was willing to take.

"I can't compromise the situation by giving you my true identity. I won't sugarcoat my intentions. What I do is dangerous—lethal. Your daughter is key to my mission, and I'll do everything I can to protect her. What I need for you to do is protect the rest of your family by letting Darby and me do our job. Don't help us. Don't hinder us."

"That's quite an air of command about you. Most fathers may accept a strange young man at his word. But I'm not like most fathers."

"I do what I have to do."

Darby's father hadn't removed his hand from Erren's shoulder. The pressure under the man's fingertips might leave bruises. The Sergeant Major may not show a lot of emotion, but he could convey his dislike of the situation.

"Interesting thing about that show." His fingers relaxed, giving Erren a pat. "Paladin was the protector of the innocent, always portraying a role. Kind of an odd show for someone your age to choose. Maybe you didn't think anyone would recognize the name or maybe you didn't realize exactly what name you'd taken?"

He knew. He'd almost chosen the actor from the series, Richard Boone, as the name to go with today, but didn't want the O'Malleys to think about it too much. Just his luck that Darby's dad happened to be a fan of Westerns.

"It's only a name." He looked the Sergeant Major in the eye. For some odd reason he wanted the man to trust him. It would be easier to leave without explanations, but he had a strange feeling that the Sergeant Major's trust was important. "Darby needs to do this, sir. And it should be with me."

Sometimes, honesty worked better than lies. Darby was headed their way and he needed to wrap this fatherly talk up quickly.

"I appreciate your concern, son, but my girl doesn't need taking care of or my permission to do anything. She was raised to be self-reliant. Nice to know she's got capable hands along for the ride."

Denny O'Malley tapped Erren's shoulder one last time

before placing both his hands behind his back to stand "at ease."

"I'm not going to waste my breath telling her she can't get involved. She'll do what she wants anyway. But if Michael's mixed up in this mess, then that's what it is…a mess. And I don't want her to ruin her career for that wastrel of a brother." He shook his head, momentarily dropping his eyes to the ground. "Daunting possibilities and odds with that boy."

Erren saw how difficult it was for the Sergeant Major to admit the information about his son. The man's Adam's apple bobbed up and down with each heavy swallow. But however Michael was involved didn't matter, as long as Darby took him to Pike's mysterious package.

"I can't really say how he's implicated, sir. Can I count on you?"

"On me?" The older man stuck out his hand, gripped Erren's firmly. "Yes, and I'll keep my boys in line, but—"

His boys—Darby's brothers. Sean was here and Michael was missing, possibly a suspect.

"But?"

"If you haven't figured it out yet, you will. Darby doesn't take orders."

"I can handle her, sir."

Darby's father laughed as she joined them.

"I came to rescue you before my father tried to get you into that balloon again." She gave her father a somewhat reserved kiss on the cheek. "Did you tell the man all our family secrets, Dad?"

"You know me better than that, my girl."

"I know what I'm doing. You don't have to worry." She left marching in double time.

Sergeant Major stroked his cheek where his "girl" had planted her kiss.

"She'll be safe. You have my word." He said the words, hit

by another compulsion to assure the older man his daughter would be protected.

Granted, he'd never been in this type of situation before. But he didn't give his word lightly…at least not to honest men.

He had to run to catch up with her. It might have been awkward making their way through the crowd, but most participants were inflating their balloons and were too busy to notice. No cops in sight. She retrieved everything from her car, including the notebook with her accounting of their activities, and nodded toward the monster truck to the left.

"What was that all about?" she asked when they had safely left the park.

"You tell me. He's your father."

"Which speech did he give you? Wait, I don't want to know."

"Is that the way he treats all your prospective boy-friends?"

"I wouldn't know. Connor brought home a girlfriend while we were stationed in Germany. The Sergeant Major interrogated her throughout dinner regarding her family history. After that, the rest of us decided it was safer to skip the meet-the-parent introduction."

"You have a third brother? Are there any more O'Malleys hanging from the eaves?"

"He's a career marine who volunteered for a third tour to Afghanistan." Her voice trailed off to a soft mumble. "Daunting possibilities and odds."

An unusual saying for a family.

"Your father wanted to make certain you'd be safe."

"I can take care of myself," she said adamantly. Her voice stronger, her fists wrapped tighter on the steering wheel.

"I know. So does he."

Whatever strange relationship the O'Malleys had with one

another, at least they had one. His lack of family made him the perfect agent. Perfect that no one would miss him if something happened. Perfect to risk everything and not think about the consequences.

Darby had too much to lose.

He reached for the charm still in his pocket. He took it out and placed the single memory he carried back on display.

"Why the dangly necklace?" she asked.

So she was done talking about her father. She could change the subject to him. He'd let her...until the next red light.

"It represents the reason I became a cop."

"It's a dagger."

"That's right."

"Wouldn't that mean you wanted to be a pirate when you grew up?" She grinned a beautiful smile. The same one she'd given him after their kiss.

It wasn't the right time to tell her his life story. Family and undercover work aside... It was time to find out why Pike had sent him to this woman. Past time to fulfill his promise and move on.

"Where's the package, Darby?"

It was obvious to him she debated what to say. Her mouth opened and closed several times, she bit her lip then chewed on it. She nervously tapped her forefinger—if there had been a pen in her hand, she probably would have done that twirly thing again.

"You might as well announce to the world that you're about to lie."

"Why would I lie?"

"Why wouldn't you?"

"Now that's not fair. I asked you first."

No grin this time. No teasing, just stalling. Again.

"And I asked you second. What does that have to do with

anything? Are we twelve? People in our line of work lie all the time."

There it was again. The slight catch in her breath. The dart of a look—definitely away from him. Chewing on her lip. Pike had said O'Malley was one of the best-trained agents he had, but man, she was totally off her game around him. Perhaps that kiss had distracted them both.

Nice information to stow away for later. Right now, she was driving north with a purpose. No meandering or random turns. She knew where they were going. She wasn't saying.

"No more games." He hated being out of control.

"I'm not playing games—"

"Give it up. I know you aren't telling me something." Was she afraid he'd ditch her after he retrieved the information? Would he? Naw. Not unless the situation turned into something more dangerous than picking up a package.

"I want to have a look at Pike's place," she finally admitted.

"Come on, O'Malley. You know the package could potentially help Michael." How? He didn't know, but he'd surmised that was the reason she wanted to hang on to it as badly as he wanted to turn it over to the DEA. "Obtaining the information will answer your questions. Or is that what you're afraid of?"

"We're almost to Pike's house. Let's take a look and then talk more about him." Her body tensed behind the wheel. She didn't lie well, but she damn well could keep a secret.

A trait that just made him want to kiss her more. Dammit. That shouldn't happen again. Shouldn't…but it would.

They'd left the city behind. The small town of Allen had exploded since the last time he'd been this direction, but it still had that country atmosphere where Sean's truck was one of many that looked exactly the same.

Darby kept her ideas close, but borrowing this Chevy

seemed to be a good addition to the plan. They drove past the last fast-food shack and into a residential area. His stomach gave a low growl. He hadn't eaten since the two drive-by burritos the previous day and the Sergeant Major hadn't offered a cup from his thermos of coffee.

And what about Super Cop over there? Food had to be on her agenda soon. No? She kept driving.

No food for the time being. The subdivision was filled with cul-de-sacs—no easy way to case a house. The truck slowed and she snapped the blinker to turn onto a residential street.

"Don't park in front. We don't want to compromise this vehicle."

"Got it," she answered, making the turn.

"This isn't a good idea." Saying the words out loud didn't make him less culpable. "The place is probably being watched. If not by the cops, then by a helpful neighbor. And if not by him, don't forget the sons of bitches that murdered Pike and are looking for the same information we are."

"It's necessary."

She drove the cul-de-sac, making the turn and passing the houses a second time. He didn't spot any obvious cars. At least not like the one parked outside Darby's place.

"Which house is his?"

"It's in the middle of the block, south side, rear-entry garage across the alley from a school parking lot. We could pull around back."

"Right. And no one will notice we don't have any kids. We can park with the teachers."

The line of cars arriving at the school was getting longer. When it was their turn to pull into the lot, the flashing sign in front said, "Welcome to Grandparents' Day." These people weren't leaving. If something went wrong…

"Aw, hell. This is *not* good."

"Pike complained every morning about the traffic the

elementary school added to the neighborhood. He was never here after his wife Marilyn died, but still complained." She parked in the lot and opened the glove compartment, retrieving the guns she'd placed there earlier. "Here, I hope you don't need this."

The 9mm SIG slid across his palm. In three efficient moves, he had the ammo checked, the safety off, and the gun covered with his shirt. Darby did the same with her service weapon. They walked along a sidewalk running parallel to the houses. Cars pulled behind them into parking spaces. At the end of the block more cars lined the street—a steady stream of parents and children.

Fields of farmland surrounded the school. Each house had an identical fence surrounding each yard with a driveway funneling to a garage door. A perfect cross-fire area.

Lots of fences. Extremely high fences.

"If I were looking for you, I'd be camped behind those six-foot hide-a-bad-guy-boards, with a barrel pointed straight at your heart."

The words didn't faze her. Well, maybe a little. She adjusted the Glock at the small of her back. Darby nodded toward a driveway. He had that strange knot in his gut again and they both pulled their guns.

Darby altered her path toward the gate and he pivoted, watching their backs, looking at a lot of civilians behind them. The garage door opened and he spun again, aiming his weapon at the empty space.

His partner stood by the keypad and shrugged. "I took a guess it was his badge number."

"I was thinking we'd make a quieter entrance, maybe through a window? If there is anyone in the house, they know we're here."

He led the way, entering the back hallway and laundry room, stopping every few feet to listen. Darby followed.

There weren't any unusual sounds, but everything had been searched. Every picture was off the wall. Every cover ripped from its cushion. Every desk drawer emptied and broken in frustration.

Plant roots were torn from the dirt, the pots shattered on the tabletop. There was no pretext this was a robbery. Photos were ripped from their sticky-backed albums. Someone had destroyed the peace of a dead man's home.

"Pike's entire life is in here somewhere," Darby said as they cleared the second bedroom and headed into the kitchen. "I feel sorry for the person who has to sort and clean up all this mess."

"That would be me."

Even the food from the fridge had been dumped on the floor. What were they searching for inside food containers? Just how big was this package?

"You're the executor? Sorry. I didn't realize you were that close to… I mean, you said Pike was a friend."

"A very good friend." A second father. She couldn't know that. No one knew. Maybe not even Pike.

He was only slightly familiar with this side of his mentor's life. He had known Marilyn from a distance, but had mourned her loss with her husband.

"This doesn't feel right." He lowered his voice to draw her closer in case someone was still in the house.

"What do you mean?"

"I mean these guys are cops. Dirty cops, but smart or they wouldn't have gotten away with whatever they're doing. They've covered their tracks and no one knows they exist. No one except us. They've had almost two weeks to ransack the place since Pike was murdered. Why search through everything this morning?"

Her eyebrow shot up, questioning his assumption as she stepped over frozen entrées and trays of ice cubes.

"The ice is still melting." There was something. That little nag. The thing he should never ignore pricked at the back of his neck.

"How long does it take for ice to melt?" she whispered.

"Out. Back to the truck." He stepped in front of her, as a *pftt* sounded nearby, breaking a window. "Get down."

Another silenced bullet broke a decorative plate still hanging on the wall. He dropped, planting his body face-first into the mess on the kitchen floor.

Multiple shots poured through the window. His new partner used his back as a springboard to sprint after the shooter.

"Darby, wait!" He watched the bottoms of her shoes rapidly move through the hallway toward the garage before he could follow. He heard the gate to the backyard slam from the perp's departure.

"Damn it, woman, you're gonna get me killed."

Chapter Five

"O'Malley, wait!" Erren shouted from somewhere behind Darby.

When he'd fallen to the ground, she'd caught an image through the kitchen window. Erren had been right about the danger hiding behind those fences and she'd been wrong to go through the garage door. When would she stop making stupid moves?

"O'Malley, there're too many!"

She knew. There were too many around her to discharge a weapon. Too many risks. Too many civilians. Too many children.

"Police. Out of the way. Stay in your cars!" she yelled as she ran, weaving between parked vehicles and others trying to find a spot.

A woman screamed. A kid cried. Parents froze, hugging their children. She had to push her way around them. It slowed her pursuit.

The perp reached his vehicle, turned and fired at least two shots. Darby hit the pavement behind an empty town car. Blind to what the perp was doing. Listening.

Metal pings confirmed additional shots. A window shattered. More screams. A door slammed.

"O'Malley!" Erren shouted. "He's in his truck. Get out of there!"

"He'll get away." She couldn't let the only lead she had to Michael's freedom escape.

She jumped to her feet. The perp was in a navy blue Ford F-150, but the exit was blocked by the flow of traffic. She ran toward his vehicle.

"Navy F-150," she said, repeating the information out loud. A trick she'd learned in the academy to help herself remember while on the run. "License FT3… I can't see the rest."

It seemed like forever, but she got a good view of the driver when he turned his head to look behind him. "Graying hair, rounded chin, no distinguishing features, longish sideburns, high forehead."

The Ford started moving. Backward. There was another exit on the far side of the school. She tried to pick the best path in order to follow.

"You can't catch him on foot. Toss me the keys, Darby. Then get in." Erren was at Sean's truck. "We don't have time for a debate."

She threw the keys, which he caught one-handed. The truck was unlocked, started, windows down and in gear by the time she put her foot on the running rail.

"Buckle up," he said.

She caught gleaming eyes through his pirate-loose hair. Clearly, he was eager to pursue the escaping ship on the high seas.

Except the high seas happened to be an elementary school at drop-off time. They hopped the curb, weaving the wrong way through the ocean of cars. She snapped the seat belt.

"Were you out of your ever-lovin' mind?" he accused, almost shouting, as if she were hard of hearing.

"Are you planning on heading him off?" She pointed. "He went the other direction, behind the school."

"We'll be in front of him when he hits the east side." He drove onto the sidewalk to avoid three cars parked on the street. And swerved again into the field to miss the parents rooted to the ground.

"And just what did I do wrong *this* time?"

"For starters—"

They hit a bump, knocking her teeth into her sinuses.

"You took after that guy without your backup."

"I heard you behind me. Watch out!" She pointed to a fire hydrant.

When the Ford rounded the south side of the school on the delivery drive, it hesitated a second before joining them on the sidewalk, facing them, directly in their path.

"This is not the place for a game of chicken," she said.

Her panic at how Erren would handle the situation fizzled as the Ford coming straight at them veered into a small ditch and made a U-turn into the cornfield, promptly disappearing within the wave of stalks. Thirty seconds later, the chase began for real.

"How can we catch him through all this corn?" She retrieved a partial ear that had flown into her lap and tossed it back out the window.

"It's not like he can lose us. This is a trail Hansel and Gretel could follow."

Erren raced the truck forward, staying on the makeshift road as closely as possible. Cornstalks slid past her window while others crunched under the tires. The seat belts barely held them in place. Darby bounced, almost hitting the ceiling of the cab. She pulled her belt tighter and did the same for her partner.

"This is entirely different from four-wheeling in an army tank with my brother Connor—which officially never happened."

Was that a harrumph or a bit of laughter? Perhaps he wasn't as angry with her now.

A dirt road emerged from the sea of green and gold.

"Finally," she said with a sigh of relief.

The hay harvester appeared in the corn-free tunnel at the exact moment as Erren was to hit the road.

The seat belt locked into place as Erren slammed the brakes and skidded to a halt with no traction, only agricultural product under his tires. His fast reaction kept the Chevy from plowing straight into the tremendous vehicle, which would have made sheet metal out of Sean's truck.

"Damn it." Erren's fists hit the wheel. "Of all the rotten timing."

They ended their Hansel-and-Gretel trek stuck to the east of the farming implement, with the Ford speeding away to the west, a dirt trail billowing in its wake.

"Maybe it's not too late. Back into the cornfield and go around this guy." But even saying the words as Erren put the pickup in gear, she didn't believe they'd see that blue truck again. On the other side of the railway tracks, about half a mile down the road, was the city of Allen and an unlimited number of Ford F-150s.

Police or rogue pursuit?

"We've avoided the cops, but can't keep following for long. So do you want to find the Allen P.D. or take this information back to Dallas?"

He slowed the truck for the upcoming stop sign. "I'm getting some coffee and a couple of breakfast burritos."

"I have part of the license and a description. We need to report what happened and get an APB out as quickly as possible on that truck. I can go through the police files and find this guy or work with a sketch artist. What do you mean, you want to eat?"

"Exactly what I said, Darby. I'm hungry and I'm getting coffee. Fifty cell phones dialed 911 back at that school."

"But we have proof. We can get help with the investigation."

"Not happening. We have to get out of here. They're probably looking for *this* truck. Once I get the package, which I assume has evidence that can incriminate these men, maybe I'll think about explaining my presence to the locals. Best-case scenario, I'll be headed back to San Antonio in a couple of days."

"So all you're interested in is delivering a package of you-don't-know-what to someone you've never met and returning to your life in San Antonio?"

"I'll be out of your hair and *then* you can make any notes you want."

He had to be joking. And what was wrong with taking notes? She was thorough, and documented what happened. So what? He said it like note-taking was a plague.

"What-A-Burger or Mickey D's?"

He was completely and totally serious. So completely nonchalant about the entire encounter it seemed a part of his natural routine. Was working undercover so dramatically different from the day-to-day workings of the police department? Did they not uphold the same laws?

"But what if he has…"

"But what if he has what?" He stopped the truck on the side of the road, pulling halfway into the ditch and placing it in Park. "It's time to stop toying with me, Darby. I need to know what's in the package and where it's located. What are you *not* saying?"

He was no longer impersonating a military pilot, and the know-it-all drug dealer had been gone since he'd rinsed his hair. Her brother was right, the chameleon called Erren Rhodes changed yet again. His eyes became harder, like slow whiskey that carried a punch once it hit your gut.

"Pike was shot in the parking lot of the police academy. I heard the shots and ran outside to find him. He struggled and told me someone would come asking for a package. His last words were, 'Trust him.' I couldn't ask any questions. I couldn't find any type of 'package' during the last week. I'd given up hope, until you came to my house last night."

His lack of reaction told her it wasn't the story he expected. He angled his head forward and glared at her through the hair falling into his face. Other than the tilt, he didn't move. She'd laid everything out for him. Well, everything except Michael being accused of Pike's murder.

"Unfreakin' believable." He slammed the truck into gear. "I need to think. Since I can't do that on an empty stomach and no coffee, I'm taking you with me. Don't bother talking or trying to plead your case. I've never really had a partner before, O'Malley, but I'm fairly certain they don't lie to each other."

"YOU SAID WE WERE GOING to Lake Texoma? What part of the lake?" Darby asked.

"This just gets better and better," Erren mumbled and shook his head, almost ignoring her.

Throughout their hour-long drive, he'd grunted or told her to be quiet. She ignored his sarcasm and watched him. Watching wasn't hard to do. Even with his face turning different colors from the bruising, his features could be admired. Of course, her brother's parting warning about not sleeping with her partner kept coming to her mind.

Often.

Rhodes was her partner. The attraction was just chemistry. A simple reaction to the adrenaline and the fact he was good-looking. Shoot…chemistry had been her only D in college. She sucked at chemistry.

"I haven't been up here in a long time. Not since Connor shipped overseas and Michael was excommunicated from the Sergeant Major's family gatherings." Her father had purchased lake property closer to home and was satisfied to see her and Sean for Cowboys games and balloon festivals.

She watched several more miles of farmland, sprinkled with the occasional oil well. "My brothers and I used to count these pumps when we drove here to camp. We always took the same route and always came up with a different number. We could never understand how that was possible."

Erren shook his head some more.

Each time he'd punched the radio on, she'd turned it off.

When she'd asked where Erren was headed, he'd mumbled something about a cabin. One of the few words mumbled during their trek north. She had hoped they'd talk more after they'd had breakfast, but it didn't happen.

Just like a man to sulk.

He didn't look in her direction. She kept watching the landscape, wondering which section of the lake he was headed toward. She'd grown up with three brothers and knew how to keep quiet when necessary. She also knew that constant, mindless chatter annoyed the heck out of them.

"Sergeant Major took up ballooning when I was about thirteen. Connor never really got into it, but Sean and Michael loved flying."

Erren's teeth gnashed. His free hand rubbed his jaw or tapped his thigh. He poked the radio on again. She imitated his movement and poked it off. He growled.

A few minutes later, they were somewhere on the north side of Pottsboro, pulling into an overgrown road where branches screeched against her brother's paint job. They were close to the lake, but not on waterfront property, with a drive wide enough for only one car—or a bicycle and one oversized pickup.

"The cabin's up this road a bit. Stay in the truck," he commanded in a broody, lone-wolf deep voice many women probably obeyed.

"No." She was poised and set to jump out as soon as he stopped the truck. She liked the anticipation building inside her. Something she didn't understand but was ready to use.

Erren rolled to a slow stop and before she could open the door, he had the handcuffs around her left wrist. When had he obtained those from her service belt?

"What are you doing?" she asked, but knew the answer. He was forcing her to stay put. He didn't trust her. The anticipation deflated like one of her father's balloons.

"I'm ensuring that you follow orders this time." He clicked the other cuff to the steering wheel. He hit the windows button, leaving them halfway down. "Your orders are to stay put."

"You're leaving me here?" He couldn't be serious. Could he? "Don't go in there alone."

"It shouldn't take you long to pick the lock." The look on his face specifically told her he knew she couldn't. "You do know how to pick a lock, don't you?"

The man was too arrogant for anyone's good. He'd get himself shot and she'd be a sitting duck. As he left the truck, the sun flashed off the dagger at his neck. She caught his reflection in the side mirror…the pirate grin was back.

Sitting in the car like a naughty child wasn't teaching her anything about field work. Erren turned ninja walking into the woods. He disappeared quickly and she couldn't hear any sounds of him tromping around.

Listen to yourself, O'Malley. You're romanticizing the situation. Pirate, ninja, lone wolf, jet pilot… He's just a guy. Just a regular guy. So stop thinking about him any other way.

That was her problem. The man wouldn't leave her head although her normal, clear-thinking brain certainly had.

She didn't need to pick the lock…she had the key. She twisted and tugged until she could get her free arm behind the seat to where Erren had dropped her police belt. A second later she was free of the cuff and the truck.

The man couldn't be that far ahead. A couple of minutes maybe, but he knew which direction to head to get to the cabin he mentioned. Tracking wasn't her specialty. It was more a Connor type of thing. She could hear his hushed voice telling her to move slowly, to look for broken branches, indentations in the sand, anything unusual. No one could move through this amount of brush and not leave a trail.

There it was…a rather large tennis-shoe indentation.

A few feet down the trail—if anyone could actually call this rabbit path a trail—she found a second footprint. The man was light on his feet, but every so often, he'd left his mark. She carefully followed, breaking through the overgrowth to a well-groomed lawn inside a three-foot chain-link fence. Two slight shoe indentations were on the inside where Erren had hopped over.

She was his partner, his backup. She retreated into the woods and walked the perimeter of the property. If there were someone here the agent didn't know about, this time she'd save *his* butt.

WALKING INTO THE CABIN after seven years, the memories rolled through his mind and couldn't be stopped. Erren could almost smell hot grease. The last time he'd been here, burnt bacon had permeated the cabin for days. Walter Pike had been a lousy cook, always talking instead of paying attention to the food.

Wishful thinking. Walter was gone.

The cabin was free of any disruption or bad cops. Erren circled back to the truck and of course, no Darby. He caught up and watched her round the fence, staying in the brush— and no telling how much poison ivy—while checking out the perimeter. At least she didn't give up.

It would be nice to retreat to Walter's chair and take a nap. Coffee or no coffee—Darby or no Darby—the lack of sleep in the last week was starting to wear on him. But his partner was searching for trouble.

He could give Darby a scare in the big, bad woods, but she might actually pull the trigger on that gun in her hand. She had rawness to her actions he didn't want to confront.

And one of the nicest behinds he'd watched for a while— even in a Dallas P.D. uniform. The rest of her curves were hidden under her windbreaker. Not completely hidden. Every now and then he got a peek at her creamy skin. No tan for that Irish girl. She'd burn in a couple of minutes, but he sort of liked the idea of limiting her exposure to the sun. To danger. To other men.

Had he gone that soft after one day with the Dallas cop?

No way. He was not seriously attracted to the woman who had lied and sent him on a snipe hunt, wasting a full day.

Oh, hell, he was. Weird thing, he wasn't worried about blowing his cover for once. This time, he could be himself. Did he even remember who that self was? Maybe it was time to find out.

Scaring her wouldn't accomplish anything. There was time for training and evaluation later. *And other things.*

Just the thought of returning to their kiss put more life into his step on the return to the cabin. Officer O'Malley had a lot of explaining to do. They were in major trouble and it was time for the whole truth. Time to cool off and pry whatever secret Darby had from her delicious lips.

He sank into the lounge chair his mentor had picked up at a garage sale a couple of miles away from his house. Walter had loved this chair. Marilyn had hated it. So the lounger found a home at the cabin.

No one knew about this property, except those invited for a private "chat." Even then they weren't told it was Erren's cabin. He hadn't been here since Walter had proposed his plan and asked to utilize the place as a safe house.

Seven years later and what did he have to show for it? A skill set any good crook would envy, a mystery unlikely to be solved and a murdered friend.

I'm going to miss you, Walter. It was going to be hell continuing alone. Nothing and no one to anchor him. A lot of questions with no quick answers.

"So, I'm assuming your cute little butt doesn't need rescuing?"

Darby stood in the doorway, gun drawn, barrel pointed in the air. She'd taken him by surprise, but he was careful not to let her see it.

"Nice of you to join me. Leave the cuffs in the truck?"

She gave the room a quick once-over and pushed the gun down the back of her department blues. Was that disappointment, dissatisfaction or a little of both he detected in the look she shot him?

"I suppose you're ready to talk," he said.

"Let's start by you telling me why we're here and who owns this place." She didn't enter the room.

Not yet. She was holding something back. He could see it in the way she stood there—arms crossed, closed.

"You think it's time for some honesty, Darby?" He rose from the chair, already missing its worn-out leather and the moment of genuine peace. "Are you ready to venture into that territory?"

As if *he* knew where the hell honesty's boundaries were. His last honest dealings were probably with his grandmother. He hadn't told her about Pike's secret operation, only that she'd always be able to reach him. In the end, it hadn't mattered. The phone call to rush to her side had never come.

"I've told you everything I know," she said. She held her breath.

A lie. He moved his hand through his hair, and her relief

visibly showed in the rise and fall of her chest. She wasn't getting any better at lying and she didn't realize it.

"Pike used this cabin when he went fishing." And for other things, like recruiting spies.

"So you think the package is here?"

"It's a possibility, but neither of us knows what we're looking for. Isn't that right?" He took a step toward Darby and she countered with one backward step, straight into the open doorway. "Start explaining, *partner.*"

"What do you mean? You're the one who left me handcuffed to the steering wheel."

"And you're the one who's never set foot in this cabin before."

"So Pike never brought me here. What does that have to do with anything?"

Incredible. Dumb. Wishful thinking.

"For starters, it means I have the wrong O'Malley."

Chapter Six

Erren turned his back to her and crossed to Pike's wall of undercover agents. Not a red-haired kid in the bunch. And one thing about the O'Malleys…they all had red hair.

"You aren't on the wall."

"What are you talking about?" She closed the door and followed to look at the pictures.

"Ten days ago, I received a message from Pike telling me I was needed in Dallas to meet O'Malley. I arrived the day after he was murdered. I start poking my nose around and the DEA gets wind of evidence that will clench the death penalty for the accused murderer."

"That can't be true. Michael's innocent."

"I thought so. My handler wouldn't tell me the accused guy's name. No details. I thought something was up when your family seemed to overreact to your brother's name and situation. A situation they didn't seem inclined to share in front of me." He pulled the picture from his back pocket. "This is a map to your house."

"Yes."

"Did Pike draw the map on the back sending me to you?"

"I'm not certain."

She held her breath for a split second too long, trying not to give herself away, but she did. Shifting her feet, not meeting his eyes. Darby O'Malley was *not* telling the truth.

"You're still lying. I thought it was time for honesty."

"Then tell me what evidence you retrieved to incriminate Michael."

"Nothing. I told you, last night was a setup. Someone wanted me to stop looking for Pike's information. What I found was this picture in Butthead's pocket."

"I don't understand. Why would he have a photograph of Pike?"

The same question had bothered him to where he'd stopped thinking straight. Jumping in before having a plan. Involving a person who shouldn't be involved. He was definitely responsible for her, pulling someone totally unqualified into an unauthorized situation.

He decided to tell her what he knew. "First of all, I don't think Beavis or Butthead were smart enough to ambush Pike. No one at any agency would tell me anything about his accused murderer or the crime scene. Before last night, I thought it was to prevent me from doing something they think I'll regret."

There wouldn't be any regret for his actions. Not from him.

"And now?" She did that cute eyebrow lift again and pulled her hair to the back of her neck. She put her hands back on her hips, and as if it had a mind of its own, her hair fell back to frame her face.

"The photograph was to entice me to the meeting or maybe they planned for it to be found on me after I killed your brother or killed you." *A kissable face. Concentrate.* "They would have framed me for the murder. Either way, it was another step to muddy the waters and divert attention from the real killers."

"How do you know that Michael's innocent? You certainly sound confident."

"He has to be one of Pike's Guys." He pointed to the wall. "It's obvious you aren't and Pike definitely said O'Malley."

"Michael is an academy washout. He's been hanging around with losers for the past couple of years. He's far from one of the good guys."

"Then why do you think he's innocent?" He was curious as to her reasons. He was willing to accept that Michael might not be the murderer. At least until he received undeniable truth that he was guilty. If O'Malley had betrayed their organization…Erren would deal with him.

"It's time you told me the entire truth."

"Pike was shot with a .38 caliber. Michael wouldn't be caught dead with a revolver. The fancier the better." Confident in her deduction, she tilted her chin, almost daring him to contradict her. "Michael's blood type was found at the scene. They're waiting on a DNA match. So, again, why are *you* certain my brother's not Pike's killer?"

"Do you see the pictures on the wall?"

"They're difficult to miss." She tapped a few with her fingernail. "Didn't Pike like his picture taken anywhere else around the lake?"

"These are Pike's Guys."

"Wait." She took her time looking at each picture, then took his photo from him and turned on a lamp. "This one is you, a much younger you. Your nose is straight and your hair is short. No wonder I didn't recognize it was you in the photo."

He wasn't *that* different.

"I was recruited by Pike seven years ago, straight out of the academy."

"Recruited for what? Who?"

"It's my understanding that Walter used people in different

types of businesses and law enforcement." They could deal with who he collected the info for later. "When he needed information, we got it for him."

"Are you saying that Michael worked for Pike? That he's undercover?" She searched the wall again. "See, you're wrong. Michael isn't in any of these pictures."

"He has to be one of Pike's men. It's the only thing that makes sense. Pike wouldn't have sent me to O'Malley if we weren't working together." Or her brother turned on Pike. The possibility Michael was guilty couldn't be marked off his list just because he liked the guy's sister.

"It's not possible. Michael would have told me."

"The DEA doesn't know what I do for Pike." Wow, he'd just taken a huge leap, and from those wide eyes of hers, she had no clue what circle he'd brought her inside. "As far as I know, Walter had never told Marilyn about the men and women on this wall. You're the first person I've ever told, Darby."

"This doesn't make sense." She shook the curls back from her face. "You're undercover and everything's cloak-and-dagger to you. For goodness sakes, you even wear one around your neck. But that's not reality. Michael did not nobly sacrifice everything—his family and future—so he could become a dope dealer for a police academy instructor."

He caught himself fingering the charm.

"Part of the reason Pike's system works is because no one ever knows."

What to say? He was back to that honesty thing again. He expected it from her. He could see in her eyes that she expected it from him. But it had been a long time since he'd done honest. What man in his position did? *He* might not, but maybe…

A cowboy. A trustworthy cowboy. Could he do a good ol' Texas boy for Darby like he did the lieutenant for the Sergeant Major?

"Pike was probably meetin' Michael when they were ambushed. They were fixin' to send me the map. My instructions were to meet O'Malley—but no where or when was included. More than likely, I was supposed to meet up with your brother, instead of you. Whoever killed Pike snatched the photo with the map from him that night, but didn't know how important it was."

"And what is the significance? It's a picture of you with Pike on a dock." She turned to the other pictures hanging on the wall. "They're all of different people with Pike on a dock. Different, but exactly the same."

"Pike used the pictures to send us messages. We each had a copy. We knew the picture was from him and that he needed to meet with us."

"Sort of an instant trust-the-messenger confirmation." She shrugged. "That was a nice old-fashioned touch. There couldn't be any other reason why these twenty or so pictures are here?"

When did he start caring if someone believed him? And did she? He was telling the truth. Her eyes studied the photos and cut to him, then quickly back. He'd been able to read everything about her, but not this.

"It's your time to come clean. The scrawl on the back of the picture, what does it say?"

She raised her eyebrow, questioning his right to know. Her serious look changed and she broke into a smile he normally would want on her face all the time. Then she laughed.

Darby laughed, holding her sides and almost doubling over. A laugh deep and…contagious. If it weren't at his expense he might have joined her.

"Oh, Erren, and just when I was beginning to trust you. Seriously, cut out the John Wayne overkill." Darby forced herself to stop laughing, but snorted and laughed harder.

Erren stood straight, his palms open to her. A classic pose

of entreaty, which seemed a bit too practiced. Darby had a little training in reading body language, too. During the past twenty-four hours she'd been too closely involved with the situation. It was time to use her knowledge and see if Agent Rhodes was continuing to lie.

"Every word I've said to you is the truth." He overstated the words, as if they were uncomfortable, forced.

"You don't have to change personalities to convince me. What you're saying makes sense. Oh, don't try to deny it." His dropped *g*'s were so obvious. "The minute you thought I didn't believe your story, you began a country-boy drawl."

"I wouldn't put it that way," he said.

Was that a flash of hurt? There was an unusual look in his eyes. It couldn't be. Erren Rhodes—if that was his real name—knew how to manipulate people. He'd gotten by her father easily and the Sergeant Major wasn't fooled by men who knew the right things to say but had no heart.

Integrity and strength were more than mere words to her family.

"You're a master at working the situation to your benefit. How are these circumstances any different?" Something she needed to remember. She could only trust him so far.

"I've lived this fiction long enough that it's a natural part of me." He crossed his arms and gave her a believe-me-if-you-want shrug. "Kind of ironic that this is the first time in seven years I've said more than two lines of truth and you don't believe me."

The shrug wasn't planned, but revealed a glimpse of a wounded male ego. Because she'd doubted him? It seemed that her Knight Errant really was uncomfortable telling the truth. He tapped his forefinger against his arm, waiting, perhaps unsure how to proceed. He took a deep breath and cracked his lips to speak.

"Don't say anything else." She raised her hand to stop him

from explaining or moving. "You're here to find Pike's murderer and you believe that person is Michael. If you want evidence to use against my brother, you won't find it."

He'd been reading her like a book since they'd met. Now she'd turned the tables by seeing through his little cowboy act. She was curious how he'd react, but there was more important information to process.

She studied the pictures on the wall, expecting some clue to jump out and guide her. The simple plastic frames seemed out of place against the real-wood panels covering the walls.

The one place she couldn't look was at him. The way his biceps tightened as he crossed his arms, the way his lower lip almost pouted. While he waited for her to speak. Very tempting, and very unhealthy. She hid the tingle that sprouted wings up her spine.

She couldn't get the taste of him out of her mind.

When she looked at him, there was something in his Kentucky-bourbon eyes that made her *want* to have faith again. Faith in herself, faith in her brother, faith in Erren.

Okay, faith or sex.

Why try to deny she loved his physique? *The man's body screws up my warning system.* She couldn't trust herself no matter how much she wanted to trust him.

Her mind reeled. Trust him or not. Believe his story or don't. Even before she could accept Michael's involvement with Pike, she needed to believe.

The concept of sweet, old Walter Pike having his own undercover agency was just too *Charlie's Angels.* It raised questions she didn't have time to answer. Concentrate. One thing at a time.

Erren moved a step closer, lifting his hand to touch her arm. She stepped just out of his reach.

"I suppose you're in a hurry to get things started? To

dig deeper?" she asked, inwardly wincing at the double entendre.

"So you believe me?"

"Your story is so farfetched." She took a step away. Not running, only moving from the intense passion now apparent in his eyes. "Don't you think we need to contact someone? Surely there's an authority who knew what Pike was up to? Someone who knows who all these people are? Someone who can help? How can you expect the two of us to get everything done or to—"

"Take a deep breath, Detective O'Malley. We have all day to determine what our next move will be."

"Hmph...as long as that?"

Somehow Erren was next to her, touching her shoulders, turning her to face him. She had to look, a small tilt of her head and there he was. All of him—scraped forehead, purple bruise on his cheekbone, a knife wound in his side and broken nose. But she could only see his lips.

"Yeah. We need to finish what Walter asked us to do." He wrapped one arm around her waist and tugged her to his body. "My gut tells me we're getting close."

The intensity in his touch made her stomach quiver. She wanted him to kiss her. For real. Not in response to taking his mind off of their situation, but to intentionally focus on her lips.

"Wait a minute." She placed her hands on his chest to stop herself from completely leaning into him. "I haven't said I believe you."

"If you didn't, I'd be knocked to the ground and you'd be hightailing it out of here in the truck." He grinned.

Her hair had sprung into her face. Erren looped it around her ear again. His touch sizzled against her skin. It was effortless to accept his hand cupping her cheek and gently moving beneath her chin, taking her directly to a kiss.

Wham.

There was nothing gentle about the fierce way he claimed her mouth. Nothing gentle in the confident way his arms circled her body. Nothing gentle in the positive response every inch of her wanted to return.

His fingers tiptoed under her windbreaker and she began to suffocate. Yearning was too light a word for what she…required. Could she be bold? Could she forget the responsibility…?

Hell, yes, she could. Her hands mirrored Erren's and soon led the way across his triceps, his pecs, his abs. She wanted skin. His skin. Her fingers demanded the smooth contours of his muscles.

She tore her mouth from his, but his lips continued their quest, leaving a shuddering trail of nips to the hollow of her collarbone.

"Take your shirt off." There, she'd said it, commanded it with a gasp, but commanded.

And he obeyed.

"Yes, ma'am." Gone was the fake John Wayne accent. His voice was strong yet held the slight twang of a natural Texan.

They broke apart long enough for him to pull the T-shirt over his head and let it fly across the room, hitting a lamp that wobbled yet didn't fall. His fingers came back to her windbreaker and began to lower the zipper.

It was time to take what she wanted. Just a few minutes to stop thinking about obligations or proving her brother's innocence. She could trust Erren for a few moments.

"I've been waiting all morning to do this," he said.

"It is kinda hot in here."

"Not nearly hot enough."

He kissed her again, hard. Not frantic, but…scorching. He tasted of the coffee and the jalapeños he'd added to his

What-A-Burger for breakfast. His mouth opened enough to make her more curious. She twirled her tongue to evoke a low moan that vibrated through Erren's entire body. He shifted closer, making her aware of his reaction.

Connecting with his skin, her sense of touch came alive. One hand wrapped around his neck, leaving her thumb near his pulse point. His blood battled through his veins in time with her own.

While moving the zipper, the backs of his fingers skimmed her breasts and she echoed his throaty growl. Her body's unfamiliar response to this almost stranger shook her to her core. It was happening so fast, but she didn't want it to slow.

His hot palms slid around her waist and up her back, leaving a fire trail in their wake. His mouth took charge, tilting her head farther back, creating another burning trail down her neck.

One minute she'd accused him of trying to trap Michael and the next she was certain he was there to defend her brother.

His deft fingers popped the hooks of her bra.

Was she certain?

"Wait."

Chapter Seven

Wait?

The word popped into Erren's consciousness several seconds before his body could stop consuming Darby's flesh and he could almost think again.

"Erren, please."

Please what? Please get her naked? Please devour her breasts with his mouth? Please take her to bed? *I'm trying, darlin'.*

His mouth pushed past the no-nonsense bra, inching its way to reveal more creamy white flesh. His tongue could almost expose a rosy nipple.

"Erren, we have to stop…"

Her hand left his neck and gently pushed at his shoulder. There was definitely another firm grip on his uninjured side, keeping him from grinding into her body.

Stop? She meant stop.

Pulling away from her was more than difficult. He desired her with a fierce hunger he didn't understand. But he did. Pull away. It was hard to catch his breath. Hard to relax… everything.

She turned her back to him, but he noticed how her hands shook trying to zip her windbreaker back to her neck. So why had she stopped?

The sparks flying between them could catch the cabin on

fire. If she hadn't hesitated, they would have been in bed two minutes ago. More likely only making it to the lounger a few feet away. The picture his mind conjured of her sitting on top of him made him shudder.

Hell and high water!

It was going to happen. He'd never wanted a woman so badly and it *would* happen…today. He had no doubts. But it was a damn good thing she'd halted them. He didn't have any condoms.

"I think I'll hit the local store and grab us some food." *And a large box of protection.* "Want anything in particular?"

"I'm not hungry."

"Erren, you know we can't." She shook her head, dropping her eyes to the floor.

Maybe not for food, but it sure seemed like her body craved me a minute ago. Did her voice sound overexerted? Maybe a little too breathy? Good, she deserved equal torture.

"No telling how long we'll be here. Makes sense to buy supplies." *Definitely makes sense to get "supplies."*

"What? We can't stay here," she said. "My brother could be in danger."

"Your brother has two armed police officers guarding him. This place is safe. No one knows about it."

"If it's one of Pike's properties, someone will eventually find it. They may be on their way right now."

"Naw." He tugged the T-shirt back over his head.

"That's your explanation?" Her voice was beginning to change octaves, higher, more stressed, angry. "This place is safe and I should take your word? Whoever is out there looking for us has been one step ahead the entire time. They ambushed you, tried to kill me, ransacked Pike's house. They seem to know about everything."

"Darby, don't worry about it. No one knows about this

place." He patted his pockets—keys were still there. His gun was still at his belt in the small of his back.

"We've been shot at twice. Men are trying to kill us. My brother's in a coma. Pike is dead. And I shouldn't worry?"

"The cabin isn't in Pike's name. It's mine."

"Time to eat, *partner*." It didn't hurt to remind Darby they were both on the same side of this fight. Maybe reluctantly, but on the same team. She'd been very irritated at him when he told her the cabin belonged to him. Maybe irritated wasn't the right word. More like furious. Or enraged he hadn't been truthful from the beginning. Surely she realized secrets were a necessary part of being undercover.

But fair was fair. She hadn't answered his question regarding the scribble around the map to her house either. And she'd started the note-taking again.

During the past hour, she'd removed the pictures of Pike from their frames and replaced each on the wall. She'd stood in front of the same photo since he'd heated the baked potatoes.

"Food's ready," he said again to break her concentration. Concentration on what?

"I know this woman's face. The twelfth recruit."

"Who?"

"Twelve pictures over from yours. The twelfth person recruited." Her slender finger tapped her chin. "I think she was killed two months ago in the line of duty." She switched her focus. "And the fifteenth recruit... This guy is an assistant district attorney, one of the better ones. He has a phenomenal conviction rate."

"Barbecue's ready."

At least she was talking to him again. He didn't care much for the silent treatment he'd received before leaving for the food. He'd thought about eating on the screened back porch, but it was much cooler inside. As much as he wanted Darby hot again—and writhing in his arms—he shouldn't.

What was he thinking? He glanced at the twelfth recruit, as Darby called her. It was possible someone had taken her down as well as Pike. Was it connected?

Sandra Baker had been a good cop. More experienced than Darby. These guys definitely knew Darby was involved, either before or after he'd led them to her house, but involved enough to want her dead. He'd made a mistake bringing her into the mix and couldn't compound that by sleeping with her.

"There's an extra nail," she said and joined him at the small dinette. "I didn't notice it earlier."

"That's probably where your brother's picture hung," he answered. "I can only assume why Pike took it down. Either it was to get a message to Michael, or to one of us *about* him."

"What sort of message?"

He shrugged, taking a bite of the barbecue. He could avoid a direct question, too. "You seem to accept what I'm saying about Pike now."

"The jury's still out." She shrugged, the gesture not escaping his attention as an imitation of his movements. "Have you worked with any of these men or women?"

"Pike brought me in once or twice." He lied. They spoke all the time. "Mainly when he needed me to help with something they were working on." He lied again. He knew how the operation worked. "He bragged on your brother though. Said he was as good as me." Impossible or Michael wouldn't have been shot. "Do you like the barbeque?"

"For the record," she said, taking a bite of the meat, "I still have my doubts about your explanations. Where did Pike get the funding? What did he do with the information he collected?"

He shoveled a fork full of food into his mouth, and then

another, to keep from answering her questions. Evading seemed easier than lying about Pike. Whatever happened to the organization, it wouldn't—and shouldn't—involve her. If she found out much more, she'd never be able to go back, and he wouldn't be able to protect her from what he knew about the dark side of being one of Pike's Guys.

"Being one of Pike's secret men would explain why a kid who had never been in trouble a day in his life could one day be at the top of his Academy class and the next resigning to avoid prosecution." She pointed her fork at him while she spoke. "Then it was an arrest for drugs with a girlfriend we'd never heard of who supposedly got him in with the wrong crowd. It wasn't him."

He'd never thought about the lies before. They came so naturally now.

"It's all part of his cover. Attempting to determine the why behind everything will only drive you crazy." He watched as Darby chowed down on the pulled pork. For someone who said she wasn't hungry approximately every ten minutes, she wasn't afraid to put it away.

"It shouldn't upset me. I've had more than a couple of years to get used to the idea. The harder I tried to get him to fly straight, the less he came around."

Behavior he understood well. "The last few years my grandmother was alive, I saw her only on special occasions. It was rough transforming back into the kid she knew. It was easier to be the undercover. At least as the doper, I knew the rules."

And didn't have to lie to my only living relative.

The look on her face wasn't pity. Nor was it envy. Curiosity, maybe? She seemed to be holding back a question. Her eyebrow arched and the unusual look was gone.

"Something's been bugging me since Pike's house. Why was the food cleared out of the fridge? They must have been looking for something small. Something that could have been hidden even in ice cubes…" The fork stopped bouncing around her fingers and dropped to her empty plate. "Erren, we're looking for digitized files."

"The old man never liked technology. He liked paper. Real files. An actual photo." He took another bite. "Thinking he put everything on a CD is pushing it. Walter was totally lost when you mentioned thumb drives, WiFi or electronic mail boxes."

"But not my brother. Don't you see—" she placed her hands on the edge of the table "—Michael loves everything new. The smaller the better. Except guns."

He had his doubts that Pike would switch his standard exchange of information for this one operation. She scooted away from the table, catching the chair before it toppled backward, hurrying into the main room.

"We're looking for some type of flash drive or a memory stick." Excitement hummed through her movements as she searched through the few books remaining on the shelves. "Where should we look? Is there a camera or anything electronic stored here somewhere?"

"Nope. Guess I'll clean up."

His afternoon priorities had shifted. Instead of getting Darby excited with the thought of sleeping with him, she was thrilled to search through every box in the place. But it wasn't necessary. He knew the drill.

"Pike wouldn't have left the files here, Darby." He carried the plates to the kitchen counter and put the containers of food in the fridge.

She stopped searching the only drawer in the living area, having found only old flashlights and candles his mother had stored there. The cabin was one big family area, no hallways, only one medium-sized square with limited furniture. Two bedroom doors on one end of the cabin with a bathroom between them on the outside wall. Nothing fancy. Remembering how many times he'd been here with his mom and dad put a lump in his throat. He'd thought about his parents more in the last fifteen hours than he had in five years.

Darby parked her hands on her hips—a tall, slender reflection in the window above the sink. "You always have the right answer, don't you? Always so sure of everything."

"Not everything," he mumbled. *I thought this afternoon would go a little bit differently.*

"What's that? Oh, you mean mistaking me for my brother?" She laughed, more bitter than a genuine laugh from her heart.

"A laugh from her heart." Are you kidding me? Dang, boy, what's wrong with your manly brain? Stop thinking like a horny sap.

"I only meant that since I cooked, *you* should clean." He turned just in time to feel her hands shove at his chest. "Hey, what's that for?"

"You're so…so…*irrr.*" She threw her hands in the air, frustration replacing the excitement from moments before.

"If you don't do dishes, just say so." He set his butt in a kitchen chair, partly to keep his hands to himself and not act upon the thoughts he'd had of getting her into bed all afternoon. And partly because he was clueless. But any male could have sensed an explosion was just minutes away.

"Oh. My. Gosh." She hit her legs with her fists. Then lightly tapped the counter, visibly showing her aggravation at his lack of response.

Okay, only seconds away. He crossed his arms over his chest, keeping his hands from reaching out to pull her to his lap.

"Why aren't you in a hurry? We know what we're looking for, so let's look."

"We need a break, Darby. Adrenaline only works for so long." He had enough experience to know Darby was ready to crash and burn. She'd had a ton piled on her in a short amount of time, and she'd been magnificent, but they both needed rest or they'd do something stupid. And in his world, stupid got you killed.

"How can you be so...so...relaxed?"

"I am not relaxed. I'm tired. This is a safe house. We can sleep and regroup here." For once in his life, he didn't want to lie. Not to her. But it was *not* the answer she wanted. "You need to calm down."

Judging from the angry look in her eyes, that was an even worse thing to say.

"What I *need* is to find Pike's murderer and clear my brother's name." The look she shot him may have thrashed lesser men. "You're acting like we have all the time in the world. God knows what could happen to Michael while we're *resting.*"

"Look, you're frustrated. And that can make you act irrationally." He propped his feet up on the chair she'd occupied moments before during their nice, quiet lunch.

"What was I thinking, trusting you for even two minutes?" She kicked the chair from under his feet, toppling it to the tile floor. "Where are the keys? You want to play it safe? Fine. Stay here."

"You need to man up—or find the female equivalent."

"I didn't grow up with any *female* equivalents. Three brothers and a father who didn't care about cuts and bruises taught me to take care of things myself." Darby paced the floor, shaking her hands, trying to put out an imaginary fire.

Energy vibrated from her. "I can't do nothing." He'd left the keys on the bookshelf next to the door. She found them, right next to their guns.

The steam in her kettle was building up to blow. He couldn't feed her emotional breakdown, but was at a total loss as to how to stop it. He had zero experience with this sort of thing.

"You stay here and get your *rest*," she said.

"We are not leaving yet." He rose from behind the table and paced his moves to match hers. She glanced away; he took another step. He tried to show he was calm and cool, even though his brain couldn't settle on a course of action. She had a gun. Holstered, but loaded. "Come on, Darby. Think logically. There's nothing we can do right this minute."

"Except *rest,* right?"

So she had seen the condoms in the grocery sack. "Give me the keys."

"Sean's truck and I are returning to Dallas. I'll find the package without assistance." She put the Glock down the back of her pants, and tossed and caught the keys.

He took a longer step toward the front door. So did his opponent. "Look, Darby, you aren't thinking about this logically. You need rest. *Real* sleep, muscle regeneration, new brain cells."

"Please cut the crap and move out of the way."

"No." He crossed his arms and widened his stance, prepared for a shove.

She unzipped her jacket to reveal the souvenir T-shirt she'd retrieved with her purse from the truck. She stretched her arms behind her head. "I can handle myself. I took Michael down in three rounds once."

"I am *not* your brother Michael."

"Afraid?" She bent at the waist, sending her cute little behind in the air.

Afraid? Hell, yeah, he was afraid. But not of her throwing a good jab or left cross. Man, she was sexy right now and that was dangerous. "Partners don't use each other for springboards following the perp. They agree to both stay or both go. And I'm staying."

She was furious. He could see it in the tightness of her lips and set of her chin. She was past hot steam and the kettle was dry—an explosion imminent.

"You don't know what it's like to do nothing. You have no emotional investment in this."

Erren stared at her, feeling like she'd sucker-punched him. The hell of it was, he was getting emotionally sucked further and further in by the minute. Now *that* was dangerous. "Think smart, not with the heart."

"Maybe they're not mutually exclusive. Now get out of my way."

"You want to leave, you'll have to get past me."

She shoved the keys deep into her pocket. "I'm not afraid of you."

He tightened his grip on his arms. If he touched her, it wouldn't be in a sparring match. He wanted that skin perfectly white, not bruised by his hand. The next time his fingers grazed her, it would be wrestling of a different sort. "If you're convinced you're doing the right thing, prove it. Take me down once, and I'll let you call the shots."

Light on her feet, Darby moved toward him to throw a punch at his right shoulder. He dodged.

"Didn't your daddy teach you any dirty tricks to use on all those military privates who dated you?" He retreated two steps. He gestured for her to come after him.

"You're infuriating."

"See, you're overreacting to my comments and not thinking clearly."

The more he spouted off, the less accurate her punches became. She threw another, and he stumbled backward into the lounger, ducking a right jab. She threw a series, and he stayed one step out of her way.

"Damn it, Erren, engage me."

She was too emotional. When she threw another lefty punch without much sizzle, he caught her hand and pulled her to his chest. Trapping her arms by her side, he hugged her. She didn't try to get away. He didn't know what to do. He didn't know what to say. He didn't think she knew she was crying.

When she relaxed against him, he lifted her in his arms and carried her to his parents' bedroom. She needed sleep. Solid, uninterrupted sleep. They both did.

But sure as a rooster woke at dawn, he was locking her door to keep himself from coming back.

Chapter Eight

Darby awoke with a start. She'd been dreaming of cornfields, miniature aliens and dodging bullets. She wanted to forget the strange images her subconscious had conjured. Familiar faces on neon-green monsters, chasing her through a maze of cornstalks that grew higher than she could see.

And through it all, Erren had been by her side, cupping her face with his strong hands, wrapping her hair around his fingers, smoothing away her tears with a soft touch.

A very weird dream.

Sitting on the edge of the bed, she searched for a clock in the cabin bedroom. Nothing. No ticking. But she'd heard...

Not ticking, it was scratching.

Wait. Rustling. The sound was real, not a remnant from her dream.

Real and outside.

She must have slept the day away. It was almost dark. Shoes? Gun? Nothing.

Where are my shoes? And where the heck did I put my gun?

Right next to Erren's on the bookshelf near the kitchen. Exactly where they'd left them during their meal.

Booted feet would have been nice, but barefoot she could creep across the floor silently. She tiptoed through the bathroom to the second bedroom, straining to hear. There it was again. A scrape against the house…or a branch. Then a shadow.

She pushed the door open without a creak and saw and heard Erren's deep-in-sleep breathing. Her partner's lap was layered with papers, at his feet a trunk that hadn't been there previously.

It wasn't the time to think about him lying there clean-shaven, in swim trunks or that he hadn't bothered with a shirt. She concentrated on the noise outside, not the body she wanted to gently awaken with her touch.

Someone tromped around the corner of the house. The gate leading to the back porch sighed a heavy, rusty groan. Reflecting the life of something old and little used.

It might be safer to awaken sleeping beauty from his lounger, but he hadn't awoken easily that morning and he might be noisy. Better to take whoever was sneaking through the back door by surprise. She made it to the kitchen, wanting the cast-iron skillet she'd seen earlier. The doorknob turned. Out of time.

Darby knelt on the floor, sinking below the counter separating her corner from the family room.

One man entered the unlocked door with caution. He took one step, stumbling in the semidarkness against one of the dining chairs.

The snoring stopped. Erren was awake.

The man had his back to her and she leaped to knock whatever he held out of his hand. Police protocol be damned. He wasn't much competition. Nothing like Erren, who had blocked and dodged her easily. This man was almost bumbling in his awkwardness.

Again she caught the man off guard, threw a right cross and he went down to the floor.

The lights flipped on. Erren was awake.

"Darby," Erren said from across the room. "Um, I think ADA Thrumburt would like you to get off his chest."

"Who?" she asked. She looked at the guy she had pinned to the floor. The fifteenth recruit. Perfectly pressed shirt, wimpy arms and a confused look plastered to his face.

"I guess we don't need to test your fighting skills." Erren set his gun back on the bookshelf. "Brian, meet Darby O'Malley."

Darby moved to one side of the assistant district attorney, careful not to put a knee in an embarrassing spot. She picked up his round, wire-framed glasses and held them in one hand while offering her other to help the young man stand. He clumsily took advantage, almost pulling her off her feet in the process.

"My apologies. I thought you... Well, it looked like you had a weapon." His "gun" turned out to be a flashlight that had rolled to the middle of the room when she'd jumped him from behind.

"Totally my fault. I should have knocked louder, but Erren expressed my need for discretion. He asked me to leave my car up the road. I'm afraid I got turned around and came via a path instead of the drive." The ADA dusted his suit pants while he spoke. He was still wearing his tie and jacket, which seemed so out of place in the rustic cabin especially as Erren was wearing swim trunks.

It was almost comical how the Dallas ADA looked like a classic geek compared to Erren, who was such a jock. An old smear of an ink stain on the back of Brian's hand seemed to confirm his clumsiness.

"But you made it," Erren said casually. "I'll see if I can dig something up for you to wear, Darby. We need clean clothes for what I have in mind. And you may want a shower."

He threw the comment over his shoulder as he disappeared into a bedroom. Once again, totally confident in his take-charge attitude, leaving her in the dark. She might just have to *communicate* with him about that—maybe with the skillet. The ADA looked at her while adjusting his glasses, then pulled them off, removed an actual handkerchief from his pocket and wiped them clean.

"I know we haven't met, Ms. O'Malley, but I'm very familiar with your work."

"That would be my brother." She assumed he was making the same mistake as the infuriating man who'd just left her alone with instructions to strip and shower.

"Oh, no. I'm familiar with your brother as well. But your interviews in the Dallas Narcotics Division have made my job much easier. You're very thorough."

"Thanks." At least someone appreciated her ability. "I'm at the academy now."

"Yes. Darn shame if you ask me. You've been a tremendous asset."

"Guess you two finished the introductions," Erren said, tossing her a shirt and shorts. "Brian, time to get started. Darby…"

Yes, he'd made a thumb motion over his left shoulder, instructing her to hit the shower. Absolutely no way. If he thought she would calmly walk into another room and let him plan the next steps without her… Well, she…

No tantrums.

No arguments.

She took a seat, put the clothes on the table and gestured for their visitor to join her.

Brian sat.

Erren pulled her chair, scooting her away from the table. "Listen, hon."

"Hon?"

"I need a couple of minutes alone with Brian." He leaned

in close but didn't lower his voice. "I promise not to keep any secrets."

"I don't believe you," she answered.

Brian looked around the room, "I can wait outside if you need a moment of privacy."

Erren placed his hand on the man's shoulder, keeping him in the chair. "That's not necessary. Darby really needs a…" He sniffed. Loudly. "A shower."

He'd sniffed her and made a face. He wrinkled up that broken nose of his and implied that she smelled. It didn't matter if she did or not. She wasn't leaving.

"I'm sure we'd all be more comfortable if I stepped outside." Brian tried to rise again.

Erren's body language changed. Instead of the relaxed jock with fantastic muscles, he became the man who claimed he wasn't lying. Everything about his demeanor tightened, became edgy. And instead of making her jumpy, she softened, unable to resist the appeal he might actually be telling the truth.

"I need a minute with Brian. What I'm discussing doesn't concern your brother." It looked as if he forcibly relaxed his features. "Please?"

It was easy to see the word *please* wasn't in his vocabulary. Had been hard for him to add, harder still for him to mean it. He tightened his abs, waiting for her answer. She recognized his tell. A very nice-to-look-at reaction, normally hidden under his shirt and one he didn't seem able to control. He was so uncomfortable telling the truth, his body reacted to it like a lie.

"Since you *asked* so nicely." She pushed farther away from the table, completely convinced she was making the wrong decision, but also at ease that she could finally see through her partner's facade. "I'm famous for a six-minute shower in my family. One bathroom, four men."

"You'll find everything you need in the cabinets."

Erren took her seat at the table as she scooped the clothes he'd thrown her and retreated toward the room she'd slept the day away in. She was making a graceful exit until she turned the knob and found the door locked.

"You'll have to go through the other bedroom," Erren said, without looking in her direction. He began his conversation with the ADA in a voice so low, the other man had to lean across the corner of the dinette table to hear.

"Six minutes."

Her partner gave her a thumbs-up and continued as if she was history. She hated to spend precious time on getting clean, but there was no predicting how long they'd be one step ahead of the men chasing them. Spending Sean's money on clothing wasn't wise either.

Very few personal items were on the lone bureau. The nightstand was empty as in the other bedroom. No pictures on the wall. The room was clean of dust and the cover she'd wrapped up in all afternoon hadn't been musty. So either Pike had cleaned recently or he'd hired someone to take care of the place.

But the cabin belonged to Erren. Perhaps he meant it belonged to him now. As the executor, he'd know. She hadn't pressed for details. It was definitely time for details.

Taking a six-minute, straightforward shower was her family trademark, especially when she couldn't shave her legs. Today would be no exception, no matter how inviting that huge tub seemed. No long, leisurely, candlelit soaks while reading a murder mystery. No bubble bath or cute feminine soap. Most of her life, she'd shared a bathroom with four men who cringed at a floral-scented or pink anything. She didn't particularly care for pink either. It was much too close to purple or bloodred.

Three colors to mark off her favorite color list. Such an

unimportant thought, but one that brought her right back to her family. She'd do whatever it took to clear Michael's name and hopefully her dad would understand.

The soap was unscented and the water pressure strong. So perfect she could bask beneath the spray and positively purr.

Concentrate on the case.

How had Erren known how to contact the ADA? "Of course, *I* was actually the one who identified him this afternoon," she said into the shower spray. "He could've called information. No deception necessary. So why the private meeting? And what was in the trunk next to the lounger?"

Erren's dark hair had dried pushed back from his face, curling behind his ears. Longer hair had been in the "cute" column for her as a teenager. On military bases almost all the young men had crew cuts to match their fathers. Most of the barbers had only one setting on their clippers—supershort.

When someone had grown their hair out, they immediately became a rebel. Immediately worth dating. With the exception of her brother Michael, there hadn't been any rebels in her life for many years.

"Grow up, Darby." Okay, talking aloud in the shower was also an old habit. She wasn't going to "date" Rhodes, but he had a killer set of abs. She'd certainly made enough mistakes in front of the agent. Including blubbering like an idiot. How was she going to live *that* down?

Cops didn't cry when they were frustrated or tired. Of course, she hadn't known she was crying until Erren had brushed away her tears as he'd pulled the quilt over her shoulders. Being tucked in was a rare occurrence after her mother had died from an undiagnosed heart condition.

Nothing like that had been allowed growing up—especially crying. Allowed or encouraged? She didn't understand which at the time. Now, she knew it was her father's way of not dealing. He was an excellent sergeant major, but he didn't understand the female psyche at all. It had always been easier for her to pretend she was one of the boys.

But she wasn't.

And the man who'd saved her life without knowing anything about her made her feel completely feminine. When his eyes brightened to strong amber, he devoured her with his hunger without laying a finger on her body.

"What are you hiding now, Erren?" she asked herself in the mirror to remind the capable cop staring back at her that her partner was alone with a man who might have answers.

She threw the clothes on—an old Dallas Cowboys' jersey and running shorts probably from the '80s. She rolled the too-large shorts around her waist, bringing the hem right under her bum, but it was a lot safer than a mere towel.

The sexual magnetism radiating from Erren would break the strongest of resisters. Hers had been in place for so long they were well established, but it was easier to imagine no barriers between them at all. Lord knew, she'd never become sexually entangled with a colleague. Yet this particular man was different. She couldn't get involved with him and had to find a way to remember she couldn't.

Agent Rhodes, *Agent* Rhodes, *Agent* Rhodes, her *partner,* her *partner,* her *partner…*she chanted on her return to the kitchen, trying to appear as professional as skimpy shorts allowed.

Brian was still seated at the table and actually rose to his feet as she entered the room. Erren had his head in the refrigerator. When he looked up to see her, the color drained from his face. He was as pale as when they were in the balloon.

"What happened?"

"Nothing." He shook his head, took a deep breath. "Everything's fine."

"Is it the shorts? I can make them longer if you have a safety pin or something."

"It's not your breathtaking legs, Darby." He dug in the fridge again, pulling out a Coke. "Want one? Or there's a chocolate bar."

"No, thanks." The comment about her legs would cause the chocolate to melt in her hand. "You looked like you'd seen a ghost or were sailing high above the clouds again."

"Let's not talk about that." He closed the subject of his fear of heights along with the door to the icebox.

"I wouldn't mind a drink," Brian said, politely reminding them both he was in the room and reseating himself at the table.

"Hand me your clothes." He reached across the small bar separating the kitchen from the living area. "I'll toss them in the washer."

"Thanks." She handed him her clothes and took a seat. When she looked at him again, Erren's arms were stretched above his head, showing off his gorgeous set of abs marred only with a flesh-colored Band-Aid.

"Are you injured?"

"How's your side?" Her words overlapped Brian's question.

"Much better. Barely hurts." He pressed the edge of the bandage covering his wound.

"What's all that?" She pointed to the papers she'd noticed earlier.

"Family stuff." He wrinkled his brow, pressed his lips together. "Just making sure that Walter didn't leave anything here."

"Earlier today you were certain he didn't." She'd like to point out that his statements had led to her frustration and meltdown, but she wouldn't broach the subject in front of the ADA.

"Don't make a big deal out of it, Darby. And I checked, I was right. There's nothing here." He pointed to the trunk. "*If* Pike had left information for me, he would've put it with my things. He didn't."

He leaned back, rubbing his eyes with the palms of his hands. The muscles in his chest and arms flexed with the natural movement. She couldn't get her mind off his body. And couldn't forget their professional relationship.

She chanted again… *Agent* Rhodes… *Agent* Rhodes… *Agent* Rhodes… She looked across the table in time to catch the smolder in Erren's eyes. She definitely needed more skin covered, but he could use a coat himself.

Erren knew he was staring at Darby's endless legs. Would she ever hide them under the table so he could see something else?

Like what, fool? Her breasts hidden by Dad's jersey?

"So, Brian, what brings you to Lake Texoma on a Friday night? You don't seem to be dressed for camping," she said.

The woman did have a nice wit. Great legs. Cute hair. Terrific body. But it didn't look like he was going to be sleeping with Darby anytime soon. Detective O'Malley was concentrating on the subject she was dying to investigate.

"I called Thrumburt this afternoon. After you identified him as a prosecutor, I played a hunch."

"Yes." Thrumburt pushed his glasses to sit higher on his nose, playing the dork to perfection. "Erren asked if I'd been in contact with Walter before his death, which I had. I've been awaiting information for a grand jury hearing on Monday."

"So the package is supposed to be delivered to you." Darby pulled the chair out and joined them at the table. "If you explain about the case, it might point us toward finding the information."

"Actually, Officer O'Malley, I was hoping you could provide me with an idea of how to prepare. I was very excited to learn you were here."

Erren watched Darby closely for any sign that she knew what Thrumburt was talking about. Nothing. Nada. Only confusion.

"Can't shed any light on the ADA's dilemma?" he asked as casually as possible. The woman had started seeing through every persona he cloaked himself in. It had to be the close proximity, but he needed to play this like a normal guy. And he had to stay natural...even though he had no clue what natural was.

"Why would I be able to help?" Genuine curiosity. She had no idea. Back to square one.

"You've been called to testify," Thrumburt informed her. "You were placed on the list per Walter's instructions."

"Could be another reason the dirty cops chose to silence you last night. They had access to the notification list and decided you need to be eliminated."

"Normally Walter wasn't as secretive with evidence and went through normal channels." The attorney sat straighter in his chair, pushed his glasses up his nose again, more excited and confident. "He contacted me the day before he was shot, insisting I convene a grand jury to hear evidence. It was imperative the witnesses remain anonymous as long as possible."

"Someone has to know what this is all about. How can I be a witness?" She pushed back from the table and walked around the room. "I've been at the academy for almost four months." She picked up his autographed baseball. Put it back on the shelf. "Any case I was involved with has been resolved."

"What exactly did you do for the Dallas P.D., O'Malley?" Erren hated being in the dark. He should have asked the question as soon as he'd suspected she wasn't undercover.

"Nothing special. I took statements, confirmed reports,

lots of paperwork for the past two years." She picked up her Glock, checked the load and replaced it on the shelf with better access.

"She did a beautiful job," Thrumburt said with evident admiration.

"You pushed paper?"

"What if we call the DEA?" She ignored his question and picked up a collectible of his grandmother's.

"Not advisable." The lawyer shook his head, certainty in those two words.

The fiery redhead was about to let the ADA have both barrels. He recognized the smoke signals she was huffing behind the lip she was biting.

"If you don't mind, Thrumburt, could you explain before Darby decides we're just shooting down her ideas."

Darby's eyes softened for a brief moment.

"I'm certain about one thing," he paused, literally looking over both shoulders, "Walter didn't trust *any* department to be involved. He said no one could be trusted."

"He's probably right. I put feelers out regarding Pike's ambush. I was set up to take some kind of ride. And instead of getting my back, my handler disappeared."

"Did Pike send you Michael's picture?" Darby asked Thrumburt while setting his grandmother's poodle figurine back on the side rail much too hard. Her impatience was clear. She wanted answers and wanted them yesterday.

"No, but I knew you were both involved." Thrumburt placed his palms flat on the table, then readjusted his glasses, then folded his hands in his lap.

Simple movements, but they seemed calculated and stiff. It was hard telling someone outside their group what was really going on. It had been for him and he knew Darby more than Thrumburt.

"Look, man, she's in this up to her eyeballs. You can tell her."

"You're most likely correct." He cleared his throat and looked at Darby. "When your brother was accused of Walter's murder, I immediately assumed the true murderers would like him dead, too. I lobbied for the case and assigned police officers I can trust as his guards."

"Great. Isn't that great, Darby?" Erren leaned back in his chair. Now she could relax, right? Her brother was okay.

"You've seen him?" She crossed her arms, hugging her middle.

"I've made it a point to speak with his doctors daily. He's recovered from his gunshot wound and been moved from ICU."

Erren heard the washer stop.

Darby waved at him to stay where he was while her lean, shapely form headed for the washer. "They've told us that much. Go ahead, Brian, I can hear you."

Brian proceeded to give a medical report. She seemed to be taking the information in stride even though she'd been yearning to know more. Darby bent over to stuff clothes into the dryer.

I could get used to seeing that every day.

Hold on. Where had that thought come from?

The same place that was still thinking about tasting her lips again. The same place that wondered if the spot at the back of her neck would still be slightly salty. The same place that still wanted to take her to bed.

"So you think Michael's in danger," Darby said, rejoining them at the table.

Damn, had he missed the conversation? What had Thrumburt told her?

"I'm not one to assume."

"Spit it out, man." He was more impatient that he'd allowed

himself to become distracted by Darby than with the attorney's evasiveness.

"There does seem to be more pressure to close the case than normal. I'm better with facts, but it does seem logical." He looked back and forth between Darby and Erren. "Now that the witness isn't monitored as closely by the nurses, he might be easier to eliminate."

"You think they may try to kill him. Where are the keys?" She stood from the table and went back to the empty bookshelves, searching. "If I can get to a phone, I can at least call the Sergeant Major."

"Hold on, Darby. Don't you think those legs may draw undue attention?" He watched her tug the shorts down to hang lower on her hips.

"You have until the clothes are dry. I have to do something soon." She returned to the table.

"We agree that Michael needs to be moved." He could be that honest.

"So you think Michael is innocent."

"Helping O'Malley won't stop me from finding Pike's murderer."

"Then why would you help him?"

He shrugged and knew it reflected how he felt. He didn't know. He'd be the one to dole out penance for the murder of his mentor, no matter who had pulled the trigger. "There are a couple of details we need to work out before we go. Have a seat."

She pushed the chair under the table, staring into his eyes throughout her entire deliberate objection to his ordering her to sit. A premeditated mutiny to any plan he'd hatched. When the wooden legs stopped their noise across the floor, she marched through the back door.

The ADA ping-ponged his eyes, watching them closely, but kept his mouth shut. If he hadn't been there, Erren might have followed Darby and stopped her from leaving. This way was more professional, if less intense.

Tomorrow. Next week. Next year. It didn't matter.

If Darby's brother were guilty…he'd be the one to guarantee Michael paid the price for his betrayal.

Chapter Nine

Erren's lone walk returning from Thrumburt's car was silent but for the crickets singing on either side of a beautiful starlit night. A sliver of a moon bounced off the lake. He kicked a rock with the toe of his tennis shoe, skittering several pebbles through the Johnsongrass lining the dirt road. The smell of rain was still in the air, due to the heavy foliage.

A lakeside walk might be the perfect end to an evening if he'd been sharing it with someone other than a Dallas assistant district attorney. Someone like a certain by-the-book cop he couldn't get out of his mind.

Darby would be waiting for him. Probably still on the back porch where she'd planted herself. She didn't have her shoes on her feet, so she couldn't go far. Unless she'd found them after he'd left with Thrumburt.

Why was this woman so different and affecting him in ways he couldn't predict? Attractive, yes. Physically, she was exactly what he wanted, but there was more. He hadn't allowed himself to like anyone while undercover. No steady women. She'd broken all the barriers he'd had in place for seven years.

Self-reflection had never been one of his strong suits. His job required few thoughts about why he did something. There was a right and a wrong. The black and white hadn't mingled to gray in his adult world, thanks mainly to Walter.

He stopped and faced the lake, taking a deep breath. Calm. Peaceful. Full of memories. He knew how long it had been since he'd let himself connect. Really connect. He'd been twelve. He hadn't been distracted by the past...or a hope for the future.

The next few days were going to be crazy. *He* was crazy for attempting this level of an operation with a rookie. There was no choice.

"Aw, hell. She's a paper pusher!" he halfway shouted into the night as he headed back. "A glorified stenographer."

Get it out now, man, 'cause once you go back to that cabin you're making a commitment to Pike, brother O'Malley and Darby. And there's no turning back.

Hell, he didn't have a choice now. He'd jumped in with both feet at her house, based on the sparks flying between them, not on the facts.

"I admit it. I want her. I like her."

And you're going to get her killed.

"I will not get her killed."

He'd made few promises in his life, but the last to the Sergeant Major was one he intended to keep. She was quick on her feet, good with puzzles and had already proved to be an asset. If it were the last thing he accomplished, Darby would be safe.

He walked to the rear of the cabin. Darby probably expected him to apologize for ordering her around. He liked that about her. He wouldn't say he was sorry, though. Not when he was right and she had zero experience.

"It's me," he said as he pushed open the rusty gate.

His partner and responsibility sat on the porch swing. The familiar smell of citronella circled the porch in the cool lake air.

"If they reported the truck at the school, then Sean and the Sergeant Major may already be in custody," she said.

Straight to it, no "howdy do" or "what did you talk about?" She needed to stop being distracted by the uncontrollable. So did he. All he could focus on was the fullness of her lips tossing him to a place where he wanted to kiss instead of lecture.

"I told your dad to watch his back." He handed her the pre-paid cell Thrumburt had purchased. "Give 'em a call. Before you do though, I…um…"

She quirked her brow at him, tempting him to kiss her and give into his wants. She dropped the cell next to her on the cushion, drawing attention to her long, creamy legs. He was one thought away from where he'd stored the "supplies."

He chose to sit facing away from the swing, almost falling through the worn-out lawn chair. The old thing should have been tossed years ago, but Pike had left it in its place. Waiting. He'd never met Walter here. The possessions in the cabin and yard were exactly as Erren had left them. It was getting harder to avoid the distraction of thinking about his family.

Not to mention the distraction of Darby. *Just jump in and get it out in the open.*

"What were you going to say?"

"I…ah…I can't remember." He laughed, a nice normal, noncalculated chuckle for once because he couldn't remember the direction his thoughts were headed before looking at her lips.

Seconds ticked by, with the silence broken only by the old swing creaking.

"So this is your dad's shirt?"

"Was. He and my mother were killed when I was twelve. We must have missed it when we packed up. I haven't seen it since the summer he died."

"Sorry. I didn't know. The baseball?"

"My dad had it signed by the entire Rangers team just after I was born."

"And the six-inch carp?" She pushed the swing, her bare feet beckoning him to look at her legs.

"My first catch here at the lake. I might have been four."

At one point in his life this had been an ordinary second home at the lake, small yet cozy. Now sadly barren, only showing the things he couldn't bear to put in storage.

"So this really is your cabin."

"It is." Her bare thighs screamed at him to reach across the small porch and run his fingertips over her toned muscles. He grabbed the metal arms and held tight.

"Who are you, Erren Rhodes?"

"Just a typical guy."

"I doubt that." She didn't bother hiding the sarcasm but he didn't let it provoke him. The rhythm of the swing increased its tempo. She was antsy again.

"I'm also the guy who wants to make certain you can keep yourself alive." He turned to her, as serious a mask in place as he knew how to generate. "Which means you follow my orders, Darby. No questioning. No second-guessing me."

"So this is taking it outside for real this time? And you win?" She laughed at her own joke.

Shoot, so much for his seriousness. The appealing laughter in her eyes got to him. He liked her laugh. Liked the way it came from deep in her chest. Not a nasal, whiny squeak that made you want to cringe. Her laugh was almost…encouraging him to join her on that swing.

Back to reality, man! He scrubbed the smile off his face.

"If you're going to be my partner—my real partner—we should go over a couple of things. Like, when I say 'get down' you actually hit the ground instead of flying after the guy shooting at us." He rolled his shoulders, stretching his back. "No buts, Darby. I've been doing this a long time."

"Yes, sir. I can take orders." She mock saluted in his direction.

"This isn't a game." His voice had risen and he got it back under control. "I'm responsible for you and—"

"No. You aren't."

"I gave your father my word."

"And I know he didn't ask you for it," she said with perfect confidence.

How could he respond? She was right.

"The Sergeant Major wasn't around too much when we were growing up all over the world. One military base after another. We didn't come back to Texas until he retired." Sadness tinged her voice as she tucked the curls behind her ears, something he'd wanted to do for several minutes. Now he could see the disappointment in her eyes. "He left four very curious minds to grow up alone…a lot. We were taught to be very independent, but I can take orders when necessary."

"I need your help to ensure your brother's safety." Crickets chirped. The breeze blew a wind chime from a neighboring yard. His abs contracted and he had to force normal breathing. "It'll be dangerous, and it may ruin your career. But you can trust me. If you listen, we can pull this off."

"I'm in."

"You don't know what I'm asking you to do."

"It doesn't matter." She stopped the swing, planting her feet on the worn wood of the deck. "He's my little brother. I'm not only trusting you with my life, Erren. This is Texas. If Michael's convicted of murdering a cop, it's an expressway to the death penalty."

DARBY WOUND THROUGH THE Parkland Memorial Hospital's halls as if it were a typical day at work. She'd been in the county hospital several times to obtain statements from suspects or criminals. She never minded visiting the hospital to do her job. For the most part visiting was okay. There were areas that smelled like antiseptic or Mr. Clean. It always smelled the same to her. Overly absent.

It had been easy to purchase hospital scrubs and white shoes at a Walmart north of Dallas so they'd blend in. She and Erren had parked the truck, traveling the last half mile on separate buses. The facility normally had a huge staff, and the shift change on a Saturday morning provided perfect timing.

She'd told Erren she'd wait for him in the visitors' area on the eighth floor. When she noticed his tall frame at the end of the hall, he stopped and chatted with several nurses at their station, seemingly unaware he was three minutes late. One of the nurses handed him a chart.

Wearing a white doctor's coat with his hair pulled back in a rubber band, he flipped through the pages and turned his back to a security camera, waving to the brunette who continued to watch him walk away.

Darby lifted two fingers, pointing to the right. He acknowledged and passed her, opening the second door down the hall. She waited a moment and followed.

"Are you crazy?" she asked as soon as she pulled the door closed. "What was that all about at the nurses' station?"

It was tight quarters in the closet where the crash cart was stored. Not much room for one person, let alone two. Erren took a step forward and was a hairsbreadth away from her.

Being close to him was driving her senses bonkers.

"Just blending in. I scored the coat on the way inside." He lifted the collar with both thumbs, showing off. "Want to play doctor?"

The tension between them hadn't subsided but only grown through the night. She'd even been able to get her hands on his chest when he'd insisted she practice giving him fake CPR. Making certain her brother would still breathe and wouldn't be harmed by her pounding on his heart.

"We have a short window of time to pull this rescue together and an even shorter amount to make it happen." Ignoring his playful "doctor" comment and avoiding looking into his eyes, she asked, "Shouldn't we go over the last-minute details?"

His lips on hers took her totally by surprise. His hands stroking the skin of her back were as much a part of the kiss as his lips. The warmth of his arms penetrated the scrub shirt, wrapping her in a cocoon of protection. She didn't understand her desire to stay secure or how this particular man could provide it. But she certainly enjoyed being there.

Her lips were moist from his caress and suddenly cool. Opening her eyes, Erren was still close because her arms had wound around his neck holding him in place. She dropped her hands to her sides, but his arms held tight at her waist.

"Hey, kissing worked when I was nervous in the balloon."

"Are you certain this is the only way?" she asked, calmer, but still uncertain. "Isn't there someone on Pike's wall who could guard Michael or something?"

"Second thoughts?" He smiled at her, damn it. A smile that told her he completely understood she didn't want to break the law she'd sworn to uphold.

"None. You can't do this without two people in his room. I also know this hospital and their protocol. I can do this."

"Great. This our special machine?" He set the chart on top of the crash cart. Fully in his element, his attitude was not only playful but excited. His eyes were bright and mischievous. "All set for hearts to go pitter pat?"

His teasing was meant to set her at ease. She hoped his infectious attitude would rub off and eliminate her jitters.

"I thought I was going to be the doctor." She tried to maintain his lightheartedness.

"And I said I would *not* be a male nurse." He straightened

her brown wig. "Don't worry about the flirting. I didn't mean any of it. The nurses have an image of me in their head, but probably won't be able to remember. They see a variety of doctors and would have paid more attention if I hadn't talked or flirted."

"I don't think you accomplished what you hoped for." *Especially with the brunette.*

"Are you ready?" The amber of his eyes had darkened with anticipation.

"Yes."

Pay attention—your brother's life depends on you.

"Did you confirm the Sergeant Major's location?"

"I used the hospital lobby phone. They're in the parking lot with the car."

"Perfect. Let me get the Medic on the line. We don't go 'til he's on standby." He dialed the cell the ADA had given him the night before.

"Erren, I want to th—"

He raised a finger to his lips.

No one picked up. Erren redialed. "Come on, man. We've only got twenty minutes."

The space was restricted and she could smell the clean, soapy scent of his skin when she turned her head to wait. She took a step back, but Erren's free hand stopped her from moving. They weren't really touching, except where his hand rested on her hip bone. And she should be more concerned that moments from now they'd be irrevocably breaking the law and she'd never be a cop again.

But right then, all she could think about was the strong, confident feel of Erren's chest as she'd spaced and reviewed where to place her hands for CPR. Or how it felt to put her palm over his heart and feel wholly alive.

"What took you so long?" Erren spoke into the phone.

"We're ready to go. You're on speaker. Remember to mute your phone unless you need to correct what we're doing."

Erren slipped the phone in his pocket. His hands cupped the sides of her shoulders and he looked into her eyes.

"Remember the conversation. Don't lie. We talked about what's going to happen. I mean it, Darby—it's all the truth. Don't lie. They'll see through you faster than dialing 911."

The man who would be hiding Michael was from Pike's wall, a recommendation from Brian and known simply as "the Medic." She'd listened to the plan through the open door while she'd been on the porch. Her inexperience wouldn't have contributed to the conversation and she'd been tired of having to hold her tongue.

Their plan was solid and she agreed it was the only thing they could do. Thank God rescuing and securing Michael was everyone's top priority. Even her father's.

Erren picked up the chart and she backed out, pulling the cart. They left the closet, turning the last corner. Erren put glasses on, stooped his shoulders and put a pen over his ear. His complete immersion into his role as Dr. McCoy gave her the confidence to be his sidekick nurse. She was saving her little brother.

And she wasn't lying, she *was* the nurse. Taking a deep breath, she dove into her first undercover operation.

"I'm sorry we're running so far behind, Dr. McCoy," she said, approaching the guarded door. "There wasn't anything to do. They got the CT Scan up and running late this morning. The lawyers were unrelenting. They insisted we proceed as soon as possible."

"If his blood pressure's been dropping all night, you should have called me, not waited for the lawyers to raise hell." He walked to the door, holding his Parkland ID up to the officer and looking at the chart. "Maybe I should call and get them out of bed at three in the morning with the results." He looked directly at the officer. "It's what lawyers deserve, right?"

The officer covered his mouth with his fist to hide his chuckle. She started to follow Dr. McCoy through the door and saw her baby brother.

"Nurse Chapel?"

"What?" Could she really do this? Could she walk into that room and pretend her brother was just some regular guy?

"You forgot to show Officer..." He looked at his name tag. "Officer Waggoner your badge."

"Sorry, ma'am. It's fine."

"My fault," she said, showing him the piece of plastic on her lanyard. "It's been a long night."

And yes. She could do anything to save her brother's life. Even break the law.

"Yes, ma'am."

She stared at a pale body, hardly resembling the little boy she'd taken care of all her life. She wanted to whisper in Michael's ear, *wake up, little bro.* His eyes would blink open, and he'd tell everyone what really happened, clear up these misunderstandings and everything would be back to normal.

Wasn't it perfect irony that if he woke up now, they'd all go to jail?

Chapter Ten

"I'll be outside." An officer stood from his chair, punching the remote and clicking the TV off. Neither officer seemed to give their assumed *Star Trek* character names a second thought.

Darby had to bite down to keep Michael's name off her lips. She hadn't seen her brother in a couple of months and had been an emotional punching bag since they'd been informed he was in custody. It killed her not to be allowed to care for him. Helplessness compounded her guilt.

Undercover work isn't a place for your emotions. You'll have to keep them under control. Erren's advice came sliding back into her memory long enough to get her feelings in check.

Erren placed his back to the open door and positioned Michael's chart at her brother's feet. He set the cell next to Michael's arm, then took a stethoscope from his coat pocket and listened to her brother's chest.

"Pulse is one-twenty. Breathing is shallow." He rolled Michael slightly on his side and listened to his back. "Absent breath sounds on the right. Not good."

Darby wrapped the blood-pressure cuff around Michael's left arm and watched the officers stretching their backs outside the door. She inflated the cuff and pretended to take her brother's blood pressure.

Erren looked at her, smiling, while he flipped the chart

open and pointed his finger down the page. Then he frowned, changing back to Dr. McCoy. "What's his BP?"

"Sixty over forty."

"What the heck is happening? His blood pressure was fine in ICU. Does he have a bleeder? A pneumothorax?" he said a bit louder, grabbing the attention of Officer Waggoner. "There's no explanation for this."

Waggoner nudged the second cop, Rios. Both officers stepped closer into the doorway, just as Erren had predicted.

"This shouldn't be happening. Check his fluids, Nurse."

She verified that his saline drip was mounted to the corner of his bed. He wasn't connected to oxygen. Thank goodness. That was the Medic's biggest concern. His Foley bag was hidden beneath the blanket.

"Pulse is fast and irregular, Doctor." She continued through her checklist of things the Medic had given to her.

"What's going on?" Waggoner asked.

Darby saw the triumph in Erren's eyes as the officer stepped through the doorway. They were buying it—and her—for now.

"Keep them out of here, Nurse." Erren's voice had gone high, showing the supposed strain of a doctor facing a crashing patient.

She crossed the room, plastering a grim, concerned look on her face—something else she had practiced in the truck's vanity mirror for miles. "I'm sorry, could you...?" They stepped backward as she began to shut the door. "Thank you."

When she'd taken her place at Michael's side again, Erren mouthed "You ready?"

She nodded.

"Get the EKG hooked up and let's see what's going on. I

want X-ray and an O.R. on standby." He took two giant steps and pulled the door open.

"When's the last time someone checked on this man?"

"Normal rounds. It's right there on the dry-erase board. They said he was improving." Waggoner pointed to the nurses' initials. "It was before we came on duty."

"He's dying now. And he shouldn't be."

"The guy's a cop killer. Maybe he's getting what he deserved," Rios blurted out.

"I'll remember you said that," Erren answered firmly. "If he doesn't make it…"

"No one touched him."

She disconnected the first lead from the EKG. The cop only reacted to what he'd heard. Brian may trust these men, but they didn't care if Michael lived or died. If she hadn't been convinced this was the only course of action before, she was now.

The monitor beeped differently. She unplugged the other leads.

The flat line wasn't real. She knew it wasn't real. But it sure felt real. Her own heart wanted to beat for her brother.

He's fine and you're not O'Malley, you're Nurse Chapel.

"Start CPR," Doctor Erren McCoy instructed and Nurse Darby Chapel performed.

She concentrated on making each step look as authentic as possible without actually hurting Michael. She'd practiced. She knew what to do.

"He's not responding," she said, letting the genuine panic in her voice bubble through. Erren's hands slid over hers as he took over the bogus CPR. For several minutes she pulled drugs from the cart, draining the syringes into the sheets near Michael's body.

Erren put on a show of working on Michael's chest.

He forced his breathing into short pants as if he were exhausted.

"Anything?" he said. "Come on, man. You can do it. Fight!"

He'd raised his voice, and she caught the cops leaning toward them out of the corner of her eye.

"Nothing," she said.

Erren wiped his brow and shook his head. He sighed, placing his hands over hers, looking directly into her eyes, maintaining contact, letting her know he didn't mean the words. "No reason to continue, Nurse. He's gone. Time of death... 6:17 a.m."

She dropped her chin to her chest, pulling the sheet loosely over Michael's head.

"He's really dead?" Rios asked.

"My God, man, I'm a doctor, not a miracle worker."

"Cut it out," she whispered. He was pushing their luck by enjoying his role a little too much.

Let's get out of here, she shouted mentally to him.

"I insist that you escort us to the morgue to get this body transported to the medical examiner as soon as possible," Erren said firmly.

"We can't move the body. We have to report and wait for instructions," Waggoner said, planting his feet more forcefully onto the tile floor, becoming just a bit wider in the doorway.

"I'm not taking the blame for this. I have a record of how late I was called onto this case." Erren over-exaggerated his movements, but still managed to seem three inches shorter. "If he was killed by an injection of some type it will be your heads that roll when we don't get blood samples soon enough."

"I wouldn't throw those allegations around lightly, Doctor." The other officer's feathers ruffled as Waggoner looped his thumbs in his belt, very close to his weapon. "Nothing happened while we were here."

"The tests are time sensitive, Officer. There might be a chance for the ME to discover what drug was used if we move now."

"You're certain drugs killed the guy?"

"It's the best theory I have." Erren shook his head. "If you'd rather wait, we'll wait. I'll just call the DA's office and tell them what happened."

Erren scooped the cell phone up and headed to the corner of the room.

"Wait. It might be hours 'til Transport can get him over to County." Officer Rios turned to his partner. "Remember what happened last time?"

Officer Waggoner became visibly uncomfortable. Darby could only imagine what the "last time" had been like. She'd been on cases where the body was lost, or the morgue was overcapacity. The county hospital only had places for six bodies. It was nothing like on TV shows.

All "in custody" cases were contracted by an outside agency to be transported across a parking lot to the county medical examiner's offices, morgue and forensics. Since Michael wasn't dead, it was important that happen quickly.

Darby watched the questions play across the cop's face. It was clear there'd been a previous problem and he couldn't afford to make another mistake.

"It's your call, Officer Waggoner." Erren managed to cross his arms, keep his stooped posture and seem like he was standing tall. His name and words might be Dr. McCoy, but his posture and actions were Val Kilmer's portrayal of the Saint.

The man truly was a chameleon. Very convincing. And must watch a lot of television.

"Call for transport, Doc." Waggoner turned to his partner.

"You should stay here, inform the precinct what's happened. I'll take the body to the morgue."

Darby tucked the sheet a bit closer around her brother's arm. They'd killed Michael for the cops…at least for a while. Now the hard part began…keeping him from dying for real.

Erren noticed Darby's nervous fingers, tucking and retucking the sheet, hiding the wet spot where she'd dispensed the drugs. He watched Waggoner stiffen, waiting. Rios shifted from foot to foot, waiting to call the events to someone in authority. Seconds passed, dragging the scene out in his head.

Erren hadn't discussed details with Thrumburt. The plan was to get O'Malley to the morgue as close to 6:30 a.m. as possible. Shift change at the hospital occurred between six-thirty and seven so things gone wrong took longer to discover. At least that's what Darby had told him. Her paper-pushing experience was a definite asset to rescuing her brother.

His turn to move things forward. What would the cops do if they didn't? He hadn't gone over any options with Darby. He rolled his fingers over the locked phone, looking as if he searched for a number, watching the men in the room who were watching him, waiting.

They'd bought the routine. They'd *wanted* the kid to die. He was a cop killer.

Hell, he'd wanted O'Malley to die before he'd determined there was more to Pike's death than it appeared. He was willing to wait for the truth. Now that he'd found her brother who could tell it.

"I need county transport for an 'in-custody' body to the ME." *Keep your voice firm and in command, Dr. McCoy.* "That won't do. Divert him to Parkland. We have a case that needs immediate attention."

Pretending to hang up the phone, he noticed the immediate relief on both officers' faces. He hated to pull this stunt on two good men that Thrumburt trusted, but there was just no other way.

"How soon?" Officer Rios asked.

"We diverted him from a run to Children's Medical."

Both men nodded. Another grim image stuck in everyone's mind. A child being transported to the ME office usually meant they suspected foul play. Guilt rushed him again for having to play the officers, but he'd use any device to keep Darby safe.

"Transport will be at the loading dock by the time we get downstairs," he informed the room. Darby visibly relaxed and he hoped the officers didn't notice.

"Baby killers are the only thing worse than cop killers," Rios said.

Darby's sharp intake of breath, caught in her throat, drew everyone's attention to her coughing. He crossed the room and patted her on the back.

Michael O'Malley's body was covered as if he were dead. His sister had slowly drawn the sheet up like she was really saying goodbye. Thank God the sadness in her eyes had a genuine reason for being there.

They were about to embark on the least predictable segment—getting past the nurses' station with a "dead" body. Erren thought through his options again. Showing his face to a group of women a second time—they'd have a much clearer recollection for the sketch artist. How could he get around that? Or should he have Darby distract them? Would they see through her Nurse Chapel persona and alert the cops?

"Just let me put the crash cart back and we'll be on our way," Darby said, pushing past him and leaving the room.

"Now?" His question took him by surprise, just as her acceptance of his lack of a plan to get past the nurses' station didn't. The Sergeant Major had warned him about her taking orders. Why should now be any different?

This was her home territory. She knew the hospital. She could do this. He'd heard her, semibelieved her.

He hated not being in control.

It wasn't a part of the plan, but he took the opportunity to slide the phone into the pocket of his borrowed lab coat with the Medic still on speaker, listening.

What was Darby thinking? They needed out of that room, out of the wing, out of the hospital. He couldn't just take off without her now. Her taking the cart back to the closet though...that was risky. Now that she'd said it, they were stuck to continue in that direction.

Erren moved aside and began unlocking the bed wheels. It was bulkier than a gurney, but it was their only choice.

"Are you sure you want to take the bed?" Waggoner asked. "Rios could find one of the smaller ones."

"I'd rather not wait. If we don't catch the transport downstairs, the body may not make it to the county ME for an autopsy today. You don't want to wait until tomorrow."

"Been there. Done that, Doc." Rios shifted his weight from foot to foot, acting nervous. "A different high-profile case missed its ride across the parking lot. We were ordered not to leave. I'd rather not go through that again. I'm not saying the body was ripe or anything. But it wasn't pleasant to be in the room."

"Happens too many times." Officer Waggoner nodded his head, thumbs still in his belt.

Erren wasn't certain what to make of Waggoner. Most of his dialogue had been aimed at making the men uneasy. *Maybe it had worked.* Or maybe he was going soft.

It was easier to walk through an operation not knowing the players and not caring about the outcome. Who cared if you busted someone for selling drugs to kids? He'd never wondered what happened after his part was successful.

"I didn't mean to accuse you fellows of foul play," Erren

told the officers, not understanding why he felt compelled to apologize. Dr. McCoy wouldn't apologize. At least not until the end of the show.

"Not a problem," Rios said.

Waggoner nodded and helped turn the bed. They had aimed the frame toward the door when Darby returned.

With a gurney.

Well, well, well… Nurse Chapel had resources. Respect for Darby and her growing capabilities was getting to him. He shouldn't be thinking about her at all…just this operation.

"This should make things a little easier," she said.

To keep up the pretense, Darby handed the officers latex gloves from the box on the wall. The foursome worked without saying a word. The beds were set together, the body hoisted, saline bags transferred and they were ready to leave.

And everything could fall apart if one nurse stopped them before leaving the wing. Just one glimpse out of the corner of an eye and they were screwed.

Rounding the first corner, they came to the point in the hallway where the staff could see them. No nurses were at the station. Erren just kept pushing the gurney straight to the staff elevators, which were around another corner.

In front, Darby pushed the button. He couldn't wait to ask her how she pulled that off. Somehow she'd diverted the nurses.

Maybe she *was* the O'Malley Pike had spoken to him about?

The doors opened. More luck—the elevator had room for the bed and not much else. The police officer stepped in last and faced the doors.

"Could you press the ground level, Officer?" Erren concentrated on keeping his voice low and soft. *Concentrate on a low-key McCoy. Low-key, boring.* If he didn't, the adrenaline rush of excitement he received at their success would cause their failure.

Waggoner pushed the button and nothing else. He looped his thumbs back in his belt.

It would have been easy to mouth words to Darby, but it was hard enough to keep himself in character. So he did his best to scowl. He read the notices about the Plano Balloon Festival and how the hospital personnel were involved with booths. Two floors and he realized how nervous he was. He hadn't been nervous about being undercover in years.

"Just curious, Doc, but what happened to your ah…your…?" Waggoner pointed to his own cheekbone.

"Good old-fashioned clumsiness, I'm afraid. I was following a staffer who tripped over the sidewalk at the train crosswalk. She fell…. I fell…. Planted face-first in the dirt and gravel. Nothing I could do."

"Great way to start your day. I've seen one or two near misses in that area. The hospital should take care of that."

"Or DART Rail. Like *that* will ever happen," Darby added.

Her natural reaction added to the believability of his lie. If he'd been listening to the conversation, he would have believed the "falling" story.

Erren had seen a near miss by one of the patients on his way into the hospital. The event gave him a believable cover for a bruised and scraped face. Of course, the nick on his neck was from an old razor at the cabin. A rough shave on a face that hadn't been completely "clean" in several years.

The doors opened on the third floor and hospital visitors stepped forward. Waggoner lifted his hand and shook his head. If it had been Erren, he wouldn't have tried to enter an elevator with a corpse. The dead body would have kept him from walking inside.

He'd tried to explain the difference to Pike once. Maybe it

was the memory of burying his parents. They had looked…
okay. Pale, cold, unnaturally posed but okay.

Blood, guts, gore…he could handle all of it. But actual
dead bodies…not so much.

Ground floor.

"Bingo," he said loud enough to be heard through the
phone. Now the Medic would move into position.

Waggoner faced him with a questioning look, but kept
walking. Darby was silent. Her grip was so tight it looked as
if she would bend the bed rail. He loosened her fingers and
watched them pinken up.

Phase three. It was 6:30 a.m. The plan was moving like
clockwork. He just needed a lot of dumb luck.

Darby had drawn him maps of the hospital, but Officer
Waggoner seemed to be familiar with the route and led
the way. Following was easier. The halls looked as if they
hadn't been renovated since President Kennedy had been
wheeled through the emergency room doors after he'd been
assassinated.

They passed the sign to the loading docks. Next hallway
was the morgue entrance. And Pike's Medic was just outside
the security door.

"Great timing. We don't even have to maneuver the tight
squeeze to the icebox." He looked at Erren as if they'd never
met, then gave Waggoner a nod. "Dallas ME Transport Team.
We can shoot him straight to the bus from here."

And that was it. Phase three complete.

The morgue door cracked, unable to fully open with the
gurney parked in front. A balding head with a comb-over
poked through the gap. "You guys deliverin' or pickin'
up?"

Chapter Eleven

Dammit! Not now.

"We're good," Erren said, blocking the view of the Medic from whoever was about to gum up his operation. "Transport's here."

"Yeah, thought he was here for the hit-and-run last night."

"We have an 'in custody' body that needs priority."

"Not a problem." The man bobbed his head, trying to see around Erren. All attempts were unsuccessful. "About half an hour then? You'll be back after the drop-off?"

"Not me, I'm headed to Children's," the Medic answered.

"Ah…sorry to hear that," the bald man said. "Okay then, later."

No "later" for any of them. Not today. He was ready for their luck to hold and to get the hell out of there.

The door closed and the Medic took over the gurney, walking toward the automatic doors with Darby. Dallas P.D. requirements were fulfilled, no paperwork, only a doctor's signature on the chart. Waggoner looped his thumbs in his belt…yet again.

"Thank you for your help, Doctor."

The officer was a nice guy. He should remember their names and ask Darby to make a note. If they ever found the package and got out of this mess, he'd lobby hard to get their records cleared.

"Thank you for being so cooperative, Officer Waggoner. I'm certain you made the correct decision." The doors swung closed behind the gurney. "I think I'll give Nurse Chapel a hand."

The officer smiled an understanding smile. "See you around, Doc."

Finally, phase four could begin—stashing Michael.

Their luck held. No one was behind them on the dock. But it was shift change and there were a ton of people crossing to and from the employee parking lot and DART Rail station. Almost home free, he caught up with the gurney before they transferred Michael.

"Let's get him inside the van and get the hell out of here." The Medic had one side covered, pulling toward him. "I'm taking him over to—"

"Don't tell us. One. Two. Three." Darby lifted with him and O'Malley's body shifted toward the Medic. "I don't want to know."

"What? The new boss man can't keep a secret?"

Darby arched a quizzical lift of her brow but left the Medic's "boss man" comment alone. She uncovered her brother's face as soon as he was inside the van. The Medic had managed not only to obtain Transport credentials, but an actual vehicle. A plain white cargo van—beat up, old, and an exact match to three others sitting across the drive.

Erren handed Darby the cell. "Time to call the Sergeant Major."

She slipped the phone into her left hand, tucking the sheet under her brother with her other. "He's going to be okay. Right?"

Her eyes pleaded with him and the Medic to make it

happen. Like she wanted them to snap their fingers and force her brother to wake up.

"Darby, your dad is waiting."

She kissed her brother's cheek, pushed his hair off his forehead and stared at them. "From the look you're both giving me, I'm assuming you'd like me to leave." She punched in a number and lifted the phone to her stubborn little ear. "I'm staying with him as long as possible. You two talk outside."

Proof that she could take orders or even listen to suggestions. Yeah, right.

"Standing around here is a huge risk to us." The Medic backed out of Darby's hearing. "It's not only risking O'Malley. Our entire operation is in jeopardy, especially with Pike gone."

"Drop it. You know we don't have a choice. That's why you're here." He watched a soundless Darby hang up and then stroke her brother's cheek, whispering something he couldn't hear. He lowered his own voice. "The family doesn't know *why* we rescued O'Malley and I want to keep it that way."

"It was too easy to get to the kid in that hospital. Anyone could have killed him. You proved he was vulnerable and at risk."

Erren's level of "uncomfortable" was off any scale he'd used before. Darby's brother was a necessity. He may be a major part of the problem or the only person holding the solution.

No matter what, Erren had decided to keep Darby close to him. She seemed to be as much a part of the answer as her brother.

The Medic nodded and gestured, waving his hands like a traffic officer. "Let's go. You guys have a train to catch."

Damn it, they *did* need to get out of there, but he tapped on the window holding one finger up. "She needs a minute."

That's all they could afford for her to stay with her brother.

"Have you thought about the consequences of getting tangled with her?"

"I am not *tangled*."

"You do realize we're still standing outside the loading dock, trying to escape with a prisoner, right?" the Medic pointed out. "What if the brother is guilty? What are you going to do then?"

He was *not* involved with Darby. *She* knew that. *He* knew that. No matter how first-rate the kissing. He had a duty. A promise.

"Pike's murderer is still out there. I know my responsibilities." And one of them was to keep her safe. They were taking too long. "Son of a…" He slammed the back doors shut, closing Darby inside and rounding on the Medic. "Get in the van. Now. I don't care who's watching us leave with you."

It would be a short ride to the next rail stop, but he received a soft smile from Darby as a thank-you. She needed the time with her brother. It might be a while before she saw him again.

"Are you thinking with that organ in your chest instead of that thing you call a brain?" the Medic asked. "She's going to get you in serious trouble."

"Why don't you keep that thing you call a trap shut?" He didn't want to admit the Medic was even close to spouting the truth. Ignore. Evade. "Where are you stashing O'Malley?"

"In plain sight at the VA hospital down the street," he said. "I'll have him in a room before they know he's missing at Parkland. Thought you didn't want to know."

"I didn't want *Darby* to know. She's a terrible liar." He pushed his hair away from his face, keeping his hands behind his head, trying to think. "Stay in touch with Thrumburt. You'll be with Michael 24/7?"

"That's what you asked. Not a problem."

"One last thing." Erren watched the other man for his reaction. "Any idea where the hell this damn package is?"

"No clue what you're talking about, man. Make this quick. I roll in less than five."

The van pulled beside the Sergeant Major and Sean, who waited at a DART Rail park and ride. Sean stood with his arms crossed tight over his chest, but met them at the back of the van. The Sergeant Major had a small towel, which he had been using to polish the broad, black stripe on the hood of a classic baby-blue Mercury Cougar.

"Paladin," the Sergeant Major acknowledged.

"Sir." Erren walked to him. "Nice car."

"I like it." He slapped Erren on the shoulder—a bit more friendly than the day before. "The kids think it's too retro. Plates were borrowed with the permission of my neighbor."

The man was different. Lighthearted. Smiling. Whatever Darby had said to convince him of Michael's innocence had lifted years from the man's disposition.

"It's a '70 or '71 Cougar?" He slid an envious hand over the shiny hood. "She got a 230 or 390 horsepower?"

"Seventy and the 390. So you know cars."

"Had a '67 Ford Ranger, found a 427 Cammer for the engine. Never got to finish her though."

"Transport is leaving," the Medic said.

Darby climbed out of the van without the wig hiding her gorgeous red hair, and Sean climbed in. Their father squeezed Erren's shoulder a couple of times in gratitude.

"I'm keeping you at your word, son."

Erren knew what he meant. Keep Darby safe.

"Enough about the cars already. Michael's set to go." Darby used that cute lift of her eyebrow and a smile to soften her words. She hugged her father like it was the last time she'd see him. Maybe she believed that. Maybe it was true. "Thanks for believing me, Dad."

"I always believe you, Darb'tagnan. Always." He pulled her back into his embrace. When he let her go, he didn't look in their direction, but his hand swiped at his cheek a couple of times before he got in the van and closed the doors. Erren touched the middle of Darby's back to remind her without words it was time to go.

Once in her father's retro Cougar, Erren raced the engine. "Now that," he said, listening to the engine rev, "is a thing of beauty."

"Where do we go from here?"

"I'm not sure," he answered. He left the parking lot headed away from the hospital.

"I thought you were the man with all the answers." Darby looked in the direction of the ambulance. "Excuse me, I forgot. Doctor McCoy is merely the man who is a doctor and not a miracle worker."

They stopped at a red light and he caught her hand in his, lacing their fingers together. The physical contact reacted with the rush he had from succeeding. Dangerous. The operation wasn't over by a long shot.

"You were great in there, Nurse Chapel." He didn't release her hand.

"That was amazing how you looked three inches shorter." She didn't pull her hand away.

"I've had some practice."

"I want to thank you for helping my family."

"Not necessary. You know I have my reasons." *No more lies?* Could he afford to be honest about his motivation before they found the package?

The highway beckoned, but he took roads heading north, following a roundabout path to nowhere. One problem conquered. The next wasn't too complicated, just undecided.

"Guess we need some more clothes and a place to lie low until we figure out where to look for the package."

"Any chance we could get into the house? Michael crashed at my old apartment a couple of times. I moved the things he left behind."

"I got inside without the cop out front knowing." He smiled at her and after he faced the road again, he realized the smile was genuine, not calculated. That reaction was happening more and more often with this woman.

"Do you know how to get there?" She patted his arm in a comforting, thank-you sort of way.

"Yeah, I can find it."

His body's reaction to her simple pat wasn't a surprise. His adrenaline level was ramped up and he'd wanted her since the moment they'd met. The desire hadn't stopped when they were in danger, at a safe house or during an actual op. Nope, the desire was natural. The admiration he had for her made him swallow hard.

That should have him running as far and as fast as he could.

He needed to keep his mouth shut and not say anything or he might admit his admiration for the great job she'd done.

Quiet had never been a problem on his part when riding in a car. His parents had taught him that silence was golden. And then he'd learned that it was his grandmother who had imposed that rule on his father. This moment was a bit different. Not awkward, not forced—just comfortable.

Darby leaned back on the headrest. She was relaxed. No note-taking, no tapping, no twirly thing with a pen. Her breathing even deepened for a minute where he thought she was asleep. Less than ten minutes and they'd be down the street from her house.

"The Medic seemed like a nice guy," she said. Her eyes were still closed, and her voice a bit heavier.

"Don't worry about your brother. He's in good hands."

"No worries, Sean and the Sergeant Major are staying with him."

"So you're covered. They know what's at risk," he said.

"Have you thought past this point?" she asked. "What do we do now? We can't depend on Michael to wake up."

The possibility of her brother not waking for some time had hit her hard inside the van. If anyone could muster him from his deep sleep it would be the Sergeant Major. Her dad wasn't leaving Michael's side.

"One thing at a time. Now, we'll get clothes, food, more rest."

"Rest?" Darby smiled.

She recognized the adrenaline rush wearing off. Her relaxed muscles matched the deep breaths that let her sink into the soft leather seat. But there was a tremor deep inside. A persistent anticipation that hadn't and wouldn't leave her alone since Erren had sat on her in her kitchen.

No, she didn't want to think, watch, analyze her partner or act like a nurse. She felt alive and wanted to do a lot of *resting* with Erren.

"You aren't in a hurry to find the next clue?"

"We need to regroup." Erren tapped his fingers on the steering wheel. "I meant to tell you that it was a good idea to look inside the frames. Pike might have slipped a map, message or whatever behind another photo. We just have to find where."

Looked like they'd be thinking instead of kissing after all. She sat straighter and stretched her arms within the confinement of the Cougar. "I still believe we're looking for digitized information."

"Are you thinking your brother had the information and tried to get it to Pike? Doesn't exactly fit our routine. Who else would have pictures of Michael?"

"The Sergeant Major, but there aren't many. We moved a lot and my father wasn't too keen on holding on to keepsakes. They would have mentioned if a strange picture of my brother had shown up recently." She pulled her notebook off the backseat and doodled to get her mind working. She found her brother's coded message and kept tracing the figures.

"We can assume the dopers tossed Michael's place first and didn't find anything since they hit Pike's place, too. Did Pike keep pictures on his desk?"

"Only of Marilyn. Nothing is left at the academy. I boxed all his personal belongings for the investigation, scrutinizing everything and finding nothing. No notes, no files and absolutely nothing about those men and women on the cabin wall. I'm out of angles."

"There's always another angle. Pike may have been compromised. One of the guys on the wall may be a turncoat."

"Twenty-one pictures on the wall, minus you, Michael, Brian, the Medic, and our deceased officer." She turned to her list of Pike's Guys descriptions, but caught his skeptical look. "That leaves sixteen leads out there somewhere."

He shrugged the way he had the night before. Ambivalent. The words doubting her brother's complete innocence didn't have to be said.

"Even if he weren't my brother, I'd eliminate him as a suspect. He was shot."

"We're missing something. Something big. It's right at the edge of my consciousness, but I can't pinpoint it." Erren tapped his fingers on his thigh. "I'm taking a pass by your house to see if anyone's watching it. Sink down out of view."

Knight Errant was acting a bit nervous. Why? She released her seat to completely lie back, disappearing lower than the window. The bucket seats were one of the nicest features of her dad's car. She flipped through her notes, page by page. Erren was right. There was a rudimentary clue here that would bring the puzzle together. There had to be. Just one small thing and they'd know what they were looking for. She revisited the images her brother had left. Why would he tell her to stick with Erren?

"It still bothers me that our pictures aren't on the wall," he said.

"I thought you believed it was to protect your identities."

"Yeah... Those weren't the only copies of the pictures. Why would *Pike* use the originals?"

"You think Michael used them?"

"Maybe." He slowed the car and searched each direction for someone who may have been watching for their return. "No unmarked police cars, no sedans. Your house has crime-scene tape across the front door. I think we'll be safe if we park on the next block. Then we'll check the inside to make certain no one's waiting for you to show up again."

She didn't need to verify his assumptions about the street. And then it hit her like a sledgehammer... She completely trusted him. No holds barred. She'd trusted him to rescue her brother and she trusted him to ensure their safety.

It had been a while since she'd wanted that type of confidence in anyone and it sort of felt nice. In spite of their fascination with the Three Musketeers, their family motto was not All for One and One for All. No, they'd been raised as independent thinkers. Letting someone else run the show was extremely hard.

The engine slowed, she popped her seat to a sitting position and he pulled into the back driveway of a house that looked almost identical to hers.

"Damn, my bike's gone. I didn't think it would be here after two nights, but I dang sure wanted it to be." Erren looked so disappointed.

Just like her brother Connor had been growing up—every time the Sergeant Major told him he couldn't keep the lost dog, stray cat or injured squirrel. Connor had always known what the answer would be before he asked yet somehow had continued to hope for a different result.

A fleeting moment of insanity painted what her future could be. Erren getting along with her father. Being on the same team as Michael. Gaining the respect of Sean. Meeting Connor when he returned from Afghanistan. Those weren't only insane images, they were dangerous ones.

Erren Rhodes was her partner and it was perfectly logical to grow to respect his opinion. Or even to trust him. She could turn to a blank page in her notebook and fill it with attributes. And again, she could flip the page and fill it with how the man pushed her to her utmost limits of restraint.

Oh, God, I actually like him!

He parked and collected their things, beginning the block-and-a-half walk to her backyard.

"I…um… Erren, I need to tell you about the map on your picture."

"What about it?"

He was on the lookout. Every two or three steps he looked behind them. He hesitated and slowed their pace before crossing a driveway partially blocked by tree limbs. He wasn't taking any chances on their safety.

She needed to take a chance on him. Hand over the last morsel of information he didn't know.

"I'm certain Pike didn't draw the map on your photo. It was all the same handwriting as Michael's."

"I'll go with your judgment. Was there a message in all that scribble?" He smiled, but it was different from his last in the car. More calculated, more predictable, more…copied. "Your brother is safe now. You ready to tell me what the drawings meant?"

"Michael's note said 'stick to guy coming for package.' We developed the code as children."

He grasped her arm, stopping her and twisting her to face him at the same time.

"That's the entire message? No meeting time? No location of the package?" The frustration in his voice rose steadily with every word. "I've been keeping you close to me this whole time for nothing?"

Chapter Twelve

There was a sharp jab throughout her body as his words struck home. Darby wanted to disappear behind one of the wooden fences lining the alley. She could hop over, sink into the dirt and perhaps be swallowed whole. It wasn't every day that the man you'd come to like and trust admitted he'd wasted his time.

The first major disappointment had been the transfer to the academy instead of undercover work. Then Michael was accused of murdering her partner, resulting in the sidelong glances and awkward silences from her coworkers. Neither of those events were enough. No, she had icing for this particular pity cupcake. She hadn't been considered good enough to be on Pike's wall of secret agents.

Pike had been her partner and it seemed he hadn't fully trusted her.

And this last reaction by Erren? Hmm…the cherry on top? That was a pretty big cherry. Dammit.

Well, she didn't consider working with the agent a waste. She'd learned a lot in the past two days. He and the Medic had gotten Michael to safety, completely immersing themselves in their roles.

But Michael was only momentarily safe. Pike's information was hidden and she still needed to clear her brother's name.

Maybe Erren was right. Maybe she was a glorified paper pusher.

"Let's move, someone may see us," he said.

"You mean someone may see you standing here wasting your time."

"That came out wrong."

"Really? You didn't mean we're exactly where we started two days ago?" The shakiness crept into her voice no matter how much she wished it gone. She walked, not because he commanded, but with every intention to brush it off. "Never mind."

She had to pull it together. She couldn't let it matter that he'd only kept her by his side in the hopes of obtaining information. And even then, she'd come up short.

They were within three feet of her back fence. He grasped her elbow and shot them forward through the gate, whipping her around to face him as soon as it was closed.

"I didn't mean it," he whispered.

"Get over yourself. It's no big deal." The hurt cut deeper than it should.

"I said that came out wrong." He raised a finger to her lips to stop her objection. "I'll take the lead checking out the house…okay?"

"No," she said and moved past him. "My house. My responsibility."

She released the safety and led the sweep of her home. Just let him try to take the duty from her.

Guns drawn, they searched room by room to verify no one waited inside. The place was a disaster.

Drawers were emptied, cabinets opened, cushion covers ripped and thrown on the floor. After they found the package, there would be a horrible mess to clean up as a reminder of her inadequacy. They ended their search in the bedroom. At least she hadn't slept with Rhodes. Nothing to clean up there.

"I just got this place looking halfway decent. I can only assume the regular cops didn't do this and someone came back looking for the package."

"Sorry this happened, Darby," he said.

Apologizing for the mess or the kissing or for involving her at all? The kissing at the hospital she understood. Highly tense situations, resulting in attraction. Simple. Psych 101. Nothing special. Except that he'd made her feel…special. It sucked big-time that she *wanted* to feel special.

Erren dropped his gun on the nightstand. He levered her hands open, and placed her gun next to his. His long fingers gently surrounded her face, engulfing her skin with warmth and vital energy.

She shouldn't look at him. He didn't deserve the emotion that he claimed he could see on her every waking minute. Not him… Not the guy who didn't want to be around her.

It was such a perfect pity cupcake. Until she looked at him.

"I didn't mean that my time with you was a waste. I didn't mean that you haven't been a help and a vital part of this operation." He touched her lips again with the tip of his finger, encouraging her to listen. "I was mad at myself for not being straight with you, including you more. I was hoping for another clue. Disappointed in the message, not the messenger."

The intense smoldering brought his amber eyes to a new heat level, holding her stare, daring her to do something.

Daring her to believe.

"If you hurt me like that again, I'm not certain how I'll retaliate."

"I can't promise not to, darlin', but I'll try."

His lips took charge, a lazy control of touching, tasting and showing. Her hands splayed his chest, easily feeling through the scrubs worn during their rescue that morning. His fingers threaded through her hair, then across the exposed skin of her neck.

This kiss held layers of growing intensity. A natural chain reaction. Lips to lips. Chest to chest. Exploring hands to exploring hands.

No matter what the circumstances, an explosion would soon occur and neither party desired to slow down or try to cap this enthusiasm.

"We're pretty sure…" She tried to speak while his lips nipped her neck. "No one will come…back?"

"Do you care?"

"Not by a… No," she managed to whisper on a long breath while his lips skimmed her collarbone.

Should she care about the possible danger? The woman attracted to this man immediately shouted no. The responsible cop tried to get a word to her brain, but the message disconnected all the sensations being generated by Erren's hands on her ribs, working their way to her back.

The anticipation was killing her.

"No more thinking," she told him.

Her loose, flowered scrub top flew across the room and within seconds, Erren was bare-chested in front of her, sitting on the side of the bed.

"When you said you knew some moves, I should have asked what they were sooner," he said.

Her partner would have to explain what moves she'd done. It was all a blur except for the hunger that kept her returning to this man. The more she fed on his lips, the more starved she became.

It was her turn to explore the ridges of each muscle defining his chest, his arms, his neck, his legs. She flattened his back to the bed, pinning his shoulders to the pale green quilt. The color clashed with his eyes. He'd look better on dark brown sheets.

She leaned close to kiss him again. To explore more of his taste and the feel of his comforting mouth. A warmth filled her body and mind. She didn't want it to end—not today, not after they finished their mission.

He moved both of them fully onto the bed, leaving her straddled across his lap. She had no doubt where they were headed. And Erren's reaction left no doubt it was what they both wanted.

She sat straighter, pushing her hair away from her face with both hands. Erren sucked air through his teeth.

Thinking she'd hurt him, she shifted to her knees to see his eyes closed in an expression of near bliss. His hands slid to her hips, pulling her back into place. Keeping her next to his hardness.

"Lean back again," he said.

She did.

His hands stole across her skin, tracing her breasts still trapped in the confines of her bra. He pushed one strap to fall over her shoulder, then the other. Darby had never particularly felt sexy before, but she did now. The way this man used his hands to skim her reserves and heighten her senses…

Impatient, she unsnapped her bra clasp, seized both his hands and positioned them to replace the soft cotton, leaning into his touch.

It couldn't be described, only experienced.

"You seem to have gotten around me. Ready to call the shots?" he whispered.

Erren opened his eyes to watch Darby guide his hands to the most perfect pair of delectables he could have envisioned.

Damn, he wanted her. Bad.

He also wanted her to keep the lead. It wasn't conceding, it was a relief. He'd given her everything she asked for…and more. Her decision. Her timing.

Oh, man, he hoped her timing was as needy as his.

Faultless globes fit into his palms, and her blush-colored nipples fell under his thumbs, easily brushed to rigid peaks. Her cute bottom unconsciously swiveled across him, feeding his ache. It was getting harder to hold himself back.

Darby brought her mouth back to his, devouring. He kissed her cheek, leaving a trail to her neck, nudging her chin from his path to her rosy tips. He nipped and tugged, wanting more. Waiting until she gave him the wordless go-ahead.

He slipped his hands under the scrubs and over the firm, bare flesh of her derrière. Hot damn, he loved thongs. Her skin was hot to his touch. He pulled her closer into him, and heard a whimper deep in her throat. A sound he wanted to hear over and over.

His muscles grew more tense with each featherlike stroke of her hand across his shoulders and upper arms.

"Darby, if you don't make a move to finish this up, I may not be there for the finale."

His words evoked a Cheshire cat grin and another arch of her back. Another pulse from them both. Another moan of anticipation.

She skated to his side, toeing off her shoes, shimmying out of the nurse duds on her way to the bathroom.

"Well, what are you waiting for, cowboy?" Her eyes darted to his own pants, still tied around his hips.

Swirling thoughts became distant memories as he watched Darby take a condom from the cabinet. After all the "supplies" he'd purchased the day before, none of them had made the trip in his pants. Thank goodness, Darby was prepared.

He was mesmerized by the beautiful woman standing next to the bed and the depth of the feelings he had for her. Caring? This soon? A need he didn't understand? He'd already admitted that he liked her. What else?

"Um, Erren?" She arched her eyebrow the way that drove him crazy.

"Yeah?"

"Change your mind?" She used her finger to point toward his legs.

"Hell, no." He lifted his hips, shoved at the pants, pulled and tugged. The pants were baggy enough and he couldn't figure out why they wouldn't come off.

"Be still a minute."

He obeyed. She rounded the end of the bed, pulled both of his shoes and dropped them to the floor. The soft thuds were followed by the silent fall of his socks before she ran a fingernail slowly across the curve of his foot.

He jumped.

"Aw, you're ticklish."

"Not really." He tried to shimmy out of the pants again. Attempting to speed up whatever torture she had planned.

"Stop." She planted her hands firmly on his ankles and climbed catlike up his body.

Her breasts gently swung across his thighs, her nipples still alert and taut. The creaminess of her skin wasn't lost on him. He was willing to wait for anything she wanted. Willing to do anything she needed. The softness surrounded him, pulling him to a place that petrified him.

The soft light shining through the slats of the blinds created a halo behind her dark red hair. Small ringlets escaped her ponytail and curled just below her ears. She arched her back and he sucked in air at how beautiful she was.

The curves of her body sank around his legs, her lips much too close to… Her tongue dabbed across his abs. She leaned on her forearms, skimming her nails across his sides. The silkiness of her breasts grazed his chest in a last push to his mouth.

He wanted to taste her, but she escaped, just out of his tongue's reach. His hands seized her buttocks, keeping her close. Then his lips caught hers, capturing her again for a languid kiss.

Darby tugged his pants and shorts down his legs, skimming her body across him the entire distance. He had a thirty-seven-inch inseam. Three feet one inch. He knew exactly how long his legs were. But the distance seemed a mile longer with Darby performing the tugging.

Back to where they started—she at the end of the bed and he lying on top of it. And yet, this time nothing was between them. He recognized the desire in her eyes, which meant no more playing around. He rolled the condom into place and invited her to join him again.

Anticipating every possible connection with her, realizing he felt complete. She was different from any woman before. He was crazy to think he could have a lasting relationship, but Darby made him feel it was possible.

He bent at the waist, snagged her under the arms, dragged her up his body and rolled on top of her. "Enough playing around."

"I totally agree."

Darby had thoroughly teased Erren and she didn't want any retaliation. His mouth nipped at her neck and she moved her lips under his again. He tried to move his body down hers, and she wrapped her arms tighter around his ribs.

"Now."

The single-syllable command seemed to be all Erren had waited for. He entered her with a careful, controlled craze. Swells from that craziness rippled throughout her lower body. Erren shuddered and his breathing hitched. It took a half minute to recover before either of them could move.

Each glide of their bodies took her to a place she'd love to stay, but the emotional impact was too intense. She'd never experienced this before and didn't know if she could handle it again.

Raw power wrapped her tenderly in his arms as he rocked into her. The crest grew with each wave until she didn't think her body could take any more. But it did. And then again.

Each caress was more intense than the last. Their journey spiraled higher and higher until Erren's muscles tightened and he joined Darby's plummet into a freefall of sensation.

DARBY MELTED UNDER HIM. After a slight squeeze secured her in the circle of his arms, she fell asleep. She was exhausted. He should leave her alone.

He'd give her ten minutes. They should get her pictures and maybe then...

Then he'd wake her and exhaust her all over again. She fit and he didn't want her to leave.

Darby turned into him, snuggling closer. He skimmed her arm with his fingertip. Soft, strong, sexy...

Why should he rush? Her brother was safe. They had no-where to be. They were secure—for the moment.

Lie here and have an intimate moment with a woman. It's been done by worse men than you.

Hell, he could play the loving boyfriend. He'd done the role a time or two. It wasn't difficult.

The real stuff was tougher. Real emotions, real honesty— the two were elusive or nonexistent—at least in his life. He *wanted* to stay and enjoy. That was the problem—pleasure wasn't in his cards. Even if they found Pike's information, the undercover lie he led wouldn't stop until he put Pike's killer behind bars.

He kept his promises.

Oh, hell. What happens if I don't want to leave her?

"Hey." She stretched her sleek body next to his, causing the sheet to dip lower. He liked that she was comfortable enough not to cover her breasts.

It was official.... He didn't want to leave.

She turned to face him, propping her head on her hand. The sheet fell to her waist.

"What's it like working undercover?" There was genuine excitement in her eyes. "Is it one adventure after another?"

"There's no James Bond intrigue involved in what I do." He did not want to talk about his work.

"I applied several times and was denied. The transfer to the academy ended my chances."

"Why are you so disappointed? So you got the cushy job, training cops. What's wrong with that? Most cops want to be at the academy. Pike loved it."

"I've always wanted to work undercover."

"It's not a life you'd enjoy."

"Now, there you go again, making blanket statements, based on what information? Why do you assume—"

"I'm just saying you're not the type." She tried to sit up, but he kissed her shoulder, keeping her against the pillow, attempting to distract her.

"I suppose that's the assumption Pike made as well by choosing Michael instead of me."

"Pike was presented with an opportunity."

"What does that mean?"

"It's Michael's story to share, not mine." The kid really had been in some trouble and Erren understood now how they'd taken advantage of him.

"I think fast on my feet. I could handle undercover work."

"There's more to living undercover than just lying." There had to be a way to express how nonglamorous his way of life actually was. "Living undercover is a nonexistence. You have to be someone who doesn't care, create a person with no memories, no morals, no anything."

She'd closed her eyes, pulled the sheet higher.

"You care, Darby. Way too much."

She crossed her arms over her middle. He understood. He'd once thought living undercover would be exciting.

"I was eager when the DEA selected me to go undercover. Naïve, wet behind the ears, however you want to describe it. Then Pike took me fishing. He pointed his short, chubby finger in my face and said, 'Look here, kid, going undercover only has three results. You either get out of police work without a retirement plan, or you get taken in by the dirty money or you get dead. It's a no-win situation.'"

He wanted to get out of bed and pace. Walk. Run. Get away from every responsibility.

"You've obviously been successful at it."

"Successful? I don't have anything, Darby. The last person I cared about was murdered twelve days ago. I have no passion left for anything except finding Pike's murderer." He lifted a finger to her lips to stop her protest. "Until I met you."

"That was some fancy backpedaling." She laughed and brushed her lips across his before lying back again. "So you have no passion? Maybe you've been undercover too long, Erren."

"There's always one more case. One more thing in your life to put on hold. One more lie that's too close to the truth."

No more arguing or discussing. He failed at convincing this woman of anything except one thing…his passion for her was real. He kissed her long and deep, gently pinning her shoulders to the bed. "My turn to call the shots."

DARBY AWOKE IN THE EARLY evening to a heavenly aroma. Eggs and toast?

"Hey. You hungry?" Erren asked, holding a plate of something above her head.

"Starved." The doctor scrubs Erren had worn were close by, so she used them to cover up. "Wow. Dinner in bed."

"And maybe something else." He kissed her loudly. "Don't make fun of the food."

"I would nev—"

Erren set the plate in her lap. A slightly burned group of scrambled eggs with a slice of sandwich cheese melted across the top graced most of the plate. It was a far cry from an omelet—or even pretty—but one of the best things ever presented to her. At least the aroma was heavenly, even if the picture wasn't quite perfect.

The toast was lightly brown, like a toaster had done its job correctly.

She smiled up at her partner and lover. "Thanks. It smells great."

"I don't claim to cook."

She took a tentative bite while he watched. It really wasn't half-bad. "Perfect."

He laughed. "Darby, you shouldn't try to lie to a liar."

So, I'm always supposed to be honest with you?

"I'll remember that."

And remember our afternoon.

Earlier, they'd hung heavy blankets over her bedroom windows to block their movements and any light. Erren had brought her dad's car to her garage so they were set to leave in a hurry, or stay until they determined their next move.

Right as usual, Erren said they needed rest and they'd fallen onto the bed for a second round of *resting*.

They'd finally slept, completely exhausted.

Exhaustion had never quite felt as sinful as this moment. Or as dangerous.

"Aren't you eating?"

Erren sat on the edge of bed. "Done. You know, something's bothered me. Been nagging at my subconscious for the past couple of days."

"Besides me?"

"Yeah." He tugged at his chin, scratching the day's worth of beard. "I was sent *here* to pick up the package."

"And?"

"And maybe your brother intended to meet me *here* and hand over the information personally. The timing doesn't work, though."

She flexed her leg muscles, sore from the unfamiliar afternoon exercise.

"Why would he instruct me to stick with you?" She put another bite of omelet on her tongue and swallowed fast. "If he was going to meet you, that wouldn't have been necessary."

"So what are the facts?" he asked, seemingly determined to find what was nagging at him. "Pike gets shot before he can get the package to your brother."

"There's blood evidence at the scene so we know Michael was shot at the same time. And if either of them had the package…the murderers wouldn't still be looking for it."

"Pike sent for me, intending to give me a map to your house." He shoved his longish hair out of his face, leaving his fingers laced together behind his head—leaving his chest flexed and a huge distraction.

"I…um… I've only lived here three weeks."

"You said Michael drew the map, but he's never been here. Did you tell him you'd moved?"

"I haven't seen him since I moved."

"Would Pike have told him?"

She shrugged. She didn't know anything about Pike or her brother any longer.

"It's more likely Michael's been watching you himself."

His eyes dropped to the fork she was using like a miniature baton, so she stopped her nervous habit of twirling it through her fingers.

"Michael drew the map sending you *here* to pick up the package, and told me to stick with you…" The solution slammed her. It was so simple. "Oh, my God, Erren. The package has been here all along."

Chapter Thirteen

Darby didn't know how to interpret the carefully guarded reaction of the half-naked man sitting on the edge of her bed. She did know that Erren had hidden every visible response to her brilliant conclusion. He wasn't acting excited, mad or indifferent. He was deep in thought about something.

Her bedroom had been a sanctuary all day, but he seemed to be smoldering just under the surface. She was ready to move, but he casually leaned across her legs, pinning her to the bed.

"What are you thinking?" she asked.

He took her plate, setting it on the nightstand and moved closer to her at the head of the bed.

"Do you trust me, Darby?"

"About as far as I can throw you." A nervous laugh escaped from her throat. He looked so serious. She could only see his mouth, wait for his body to connect with hers...and feel totally guilty she wasn't searching for the package.

"The information could be in the next room," she said, in an attempt to distract him—Michael wasn't safe yet. That smoldering look had been replaced with outright passion. Very hard to ignore.

"I need you to trust me, hon." He spoke, but seemed more intent on touching her legs and moving his hand up to her hip. The heat of his flesh burned through the thin material.

"For some illogical reason, I've trusted you this far. If it's about Michael, you can just tell me."

"Whatever we find, remember that."

He towed her into his arms and kissed her slowly. The heat penetrated everywhere. The tingles felt deep in her belly and shot straight through her chest. A mixture of tough guy and tender lover. A lasting kiss worthy of any movie farewell.

Why him? Why this feeling? There wasn't time to think about it as the kiss ended and he looked into her eyes. He saw past whatever barrier had been there for other men. He saw… her.

Totally confused, she didn't know why the conversation had turned to trusting him instead of where the package might be found. But then, maybe he felt guilty. "If this is about us sleeping together, I don't have any regrets."

"Neither do I. Just remember, okay?"

She nodded even though she still didn't know why she was agreeing. Whatever the problem was, she needed to march into the other room and find Michael's picture and the next clue.

"Guess it's time to go back to work," he said. "I saw the pictures in the other bedroom. You ready to look through the mess now?"

"Not a problem." Had he kissed her to distract her? If so, it was a nice habit to develop. And no, she wouldn't be all right seeing the little bit of family history she had left, broken and torn all over the floor. But she'd handle it…for Michael.

Erren stood and she immediately missed his touch.

His scrubs hung low on his hips, leaving nothing to her imagination after this afternoon. If they could find the package and deliver the information—maybe without distractions—something longer than one night could develop between them.

It was a much better plan.

It wasn't her favorite plan. She'd prefer spending an unlimited time secluded in this candlelit room with her new lover.

"Michael's stuff is in the garage." She sighed, forcing the sexy images from her mind. "You saw my photos in the front bedroom."

Would she ever be ready to look through any of it? When she'd found the ruined photos, her first thought was of losing her mother again.

"Since Michael hasn't been here at the house, let's check his box of things first." He stretched his arms above his head, a casual move that shouldn't have mesmerized her.

She stared, loving the way the candlelight flickering across his tanned skin turned him into a golden Adonis. She needed to get him into some clothes, before she lost control. "Michael could have brought the package here any time. He picked the lock at my old apartment once."

"Or he could've hidden it with your things prior to your move."

"I can't believe we've been running around in circles for two days and the package was here all along."

"Why? Neither of us knew anything about the situation. Or each other." He gestured for her to get up. "I think we've done okay, all things considered."

"The pieces were there. I can't understand why it took me so long to fit them together. What if it's *not* here?"

"You sure have a crazy lack of self-esteem, Detective O'Malley. Weren't you the one who just figured out we should be looking *here* for the information? Are you coming?" He waited by the door. "If it's not, we'll find another clue. Period. That's the way things work."

She jumped from the bed, suddenly conscious of her bare bottom. Maybe it had been his calling her "detective." Maybe it was just thinking about clearing her brother. She pulled out clean underwear, jeans, a T-shirt, turned her back and pulled on the clothes. She couldn't search for Michael's picture wearing a thong.

When she faced him again, the pants had slipped lower on his hips, the definition of each muscle calling to be caressed. Honestly, she had to get him covered, or she'd never be able to focus on anything else.

"I stored the box with Michael's stuff out in the garage." She led the way, leaving the lights off in the kitchen. "The box was in the corner by the hot-water heater. There should at least be a shirt we can grab for you to wear."

"You've seen me with my shirt off." He was following close behind her. When she stopped to open the door, he trapped her in his arms against it. He leaned in close, whispering next to her ear, nipping her lobe. "There's no reason to be uptight now."

He continued his nibbling down her neck and she continued to melt.

"We…um…" She halfway pushed at his shoulders. "We need to find Pike's information."

"Sure. I'll get the box." He reached around her and opened the door. "By the hot-water heater?"

"Yeah, it's not big."

He stepped into the darkness and she dropped her head against the wall. He was a definite distraction. Michael may be safe, but it was only temporary. She had to find Pike's information and make certain it was delivered to Thrumburt or whoever else may need it. No matter how much she wanted to stay and enjoy time with Erren, her first responsibility was to her family.

"We should take it back to the bedroom," he said, leading the way.

"When I moved, this box had a set of clothes, a couple of CDs and books. Nothing else," she said, back in the bedroom.

They were using a candle and flashlight to see, casting strange shadows on the walls. Erren set the box on the floor and popped the tape, looking inside.

"Looks like the same stuff. Man, is that a Bowling for Soup shirt? Nice band. I won't mind hanging in that for a while." He popped his head and arms through the opening.

So maybe she could focus now.

They each picked up a book and thumbed through the pages.

"And the pants?" she asked as casually as she could manage.

"Probably a fit." He leaned in for a quick kiss. "Are you worried you won't be able to keep your paws off me?"

There was nothing quick about her reaction to him. Each touch created a slow burn of need from somewhere that had never been tapped before. It built into a five-alarm fire. And she called upon those imaginary fire trucks to put out the flames.

She had to. Her family depended on her.

There wasn't a microbe left in the box. She ignored his comment—and the kiss—and handed him the CD cases. "I listened to this music before I moved. Pike's info isn't here. You saw the box of pictures in the front bedroom."

"I'll get it," he said. "Cut the light. No need to notify anyone watching the place we're here."

"We can't move that mess." She turned the flashlight off and followed—glad she couldn't see much of his muscular outline. She'd love to stay in bed to look at family pictures instead of sleuthing through them for clues. Getting to know this man under normal circumstances was very appealing.

It had been nice to forget the responsibility for a little while, as she had this afternoon. The dreams she'd had after they'd made love had been much more enjoyable than the little green monsters she'd imagined yesterday. If she could hold those monsters at bay until Michael could tell the truth, she might be able to dream a bit more with a certain DEA agent.

"That's a lot of pictures," he said.

Each photograph was special. She'd packed all of her things from the apartment and knew exactly how each had been wrapped in paper, tucked safely away, to keep the frames from being scratched and the memories intact.

"It looks like someone was angry when they didn't find what they were looking for," she said.

The box had been upended. Broken glass, bent frames, a torn photograph rudely glared at her from the floor. Pieces of her existence were carelessly scattered from one corner to another.

A picture of the O'Malley children, dressed in their Three Musketeer terry-cloth capes and stick swords, lay under the first layer of her life.

"Michael said, 'stick to man.' He assumed you would ask for the picture." She lifted the solid wooden frame her father had put together from their pretend swords. "This is what he meant. You're the man and the frame is the stick."

"It's not the right photo."

"I bet it is." She flipped the frame over and the backing protecting the picture had been sliced and taped. She pulled the brown paper away and the picture of her brother was stuffed behind the front photo. Walter stood on a wooden dock with her baby brother beside him. His red hair was short from his time at the academy.

"He really is one of Pike's Guys." The picture confirmed all the faith she'd had in her little brother. "He gave up his family in order to bring down drug dealers and dirty cops."

"Let's get back to some light before you remove the picture so we can see everything."

Secret Agent Man tried to contain his impatience, but it radiated from each movement he made. No huffing and puffing, but a definite "hurry up" and she loved that he tried to stuff his hands into nonexistent pockets on the scrubs. He ended up interlocking his fingers behind his head.

"No more torture." She removed the picture then the cardboard and two phone cards were revealed—a microSD and a SIM card. "It can't be that simple."

"Great, another freakin' delay." Erren sounded frustrated and wasn't bothering to hide it. "We don't have a way to read the data."

"Wait a minute. Sean found an SD/USB adapter on the floor when we were painting. I didn't think anything of it at the time. Hold this and stay here." She placed the small cards in the palm of his hand. "Where did Sean put that thing? Oh yeah, the kitchen drawer."

It took a minute in the dark, but the light from the alley helped find the bright green adapter. "Got it."

Without seeing the information on the card, a feeling of relief filled her entire body. Followed quickly by a moment of disappointment that her time with her new partner was close to an end. It built hard and fast, creating a lump in her throat that she pushed aside.

Her desires didn't matter. Michael may never wake up. Pike was dead.

She returned to the bedroom within seconds, staring at Erren who sat on the bed, holding the cards in one palm.

"This is it. It's almost over." She took the cards from him.

"So...let's see." Erren slapped his hands, rubbing his palms together. "Where can we find a computer? I'm assuming yours is no longer here after the search and seizure."

"Not so fast, cowboy. We can view everything on that prepaid cell Brian gave us."

"You're a techno-geek and a pencil pusher. Good to know."

She scooped the phone from the nightstand and they both sat on the edge of her new queen-size bed. It was either the bed or the floor.

Once the SD card was in the phone, she said, "Are you ready to apologize?"

"Why should I?"

She found and opened the photos application. "Because I'm about to prove that Michael is innocent."

The first photos were of people she didn't know—almost normal pictures as far as she could tell. A girl, several men, nightlife…things any person would have on their cell phone. And then there were pictures of drugs being used.

She thumbed through and Erren watched without a word.

Fifteen or sixteen pictures went by and she thought she might have to apologize to Erren for her assumptions about Michael's innocence. From the partying he'd documented, it seemed clear he was into the drug scene.

Then pay dirt. She zoomed in on the JPEG and held it up for Erren to look closely.

"We need to print these pictures so they're easier to read, but that's an evidence inventory sheet."

"How do you know?"

"That's my handwriting. I took witness statements and verified evidence. I processed the drug busts and substantiated proof for prosecution." She advanced to the next picture. "That… That's not right."

"What?"

"I remember this case, and the numbers on this document aren't the same as what I documented in the files. The drug bust was huge and this states it was minor."

"Are you sure?"

"Yes. They underestimated the amount they confiscated. I confirmed the changes with the DEA. It was one of the last cases I was involved with, just before my transfer to the academy."

He jumped from the bed. "Where are your copies?"

"I filed everything with the department."

He grinned, lifted his brows and nodded his head. "After two days of your note-taking, I am assuming you have backup copies of everything you filed. Backup copies that aren't stored at the department."

"Sure, I burned CDs, but—"

"Don't you see, Darby?" There was no mistaking the excitement in his voice or his expression. "Pike knew. This is why he transferred you to the academy. I'm not here to protect pictures on an SD card. Your brother found out they were planning to eliminate the evidence. I was brought here to protect you."

"I'm not following." She held up the phone with one hand and tapped on it with her other forefinger. "You're here to deliver the package to the ADA."

"Officer O'Malley, *you* are the package."

Chapter Fourteen

"You're crazy."

Erren watched as Darby shook her head, thumbing more rapidly through the pictures on the phone. His handler's face came up again and again. She didn't know the significance of the man's connection to the DEA. But their can of worms had just exploded.

Hell, could this get any worse?

"Not crazy. You've been shot at, chased down and your partner is dead. I'm surprised we didn't think of this before. Makes more sense than anything else on this bizarre case."

Erren turned her in his arms and stroked her cheek with his thumb. "I'll keep you safe. I promise."

"I'm not worried about me. There has to be more. Something to prove Michael's innocence, not just copies of these files that connect cops to stealing drugs. This can't be everything. We haven't looked in the right place."

He wanted to brush the worry lines from her brow. Tell her everything was going to be great. He couldn't force the words. They were lies and he was tired of not being truthful—at least with her.

"These guys are good. You know it. I know it. Pike and Michael knew it. I'm going to make sure you make it to the witness stand alive."

He shoved her toward the bathroom, stealing the phone

from her hand. "Now, get ready and I'll take you and Michael's evidence to Thrumburt."

"I think you're wrong," she said.

"You don't or you'd be arguing." He smiled, knowing her brain was running through a list of possible things to discuss. "We aren't arguing."

"I could come up with something…" She threw him a tempting smile. "Or you could help me wash my back."

"If I get you wet and naked, we'll never leave. Go." He kissed her nose, and gently pushed her—shaking head and toned body—through the bathroom door. Once the water came on, Erren leaned his forehead against the cool wood.

His partner was waiting in the shower—for him—convinced he was wrong.

He wasn't wrong.

Joining her and forgetting about the world for a few more hours would only put her at greater risk. He couldn't do it. He sighed and looked through the pictures on the phone card.

Staring straight into the camera was his Dallas DEA handler. The man who'd set him up with Beavis and Butthead. Probably the guy who'd caught him in the alley cross fire and had shot the drug dealer dead when the cops had made the scene.

Proof positive the drug operation went deeper than just dirty cops. The dirt spread at least through the DEA. And it would be a hell of a mess to clean up.

So why couldn't he tell her?

How do you tell a woman whose entire life is her family and love of police work that she most likely would have to give all that up when she testified? Her sense of duty would force her to testify. He didn't doubt that.

He'd seen it several times in his work. He'd convinced witnesses himself. Testify against the big, bad drug cartel and the government will give you a new life.

WitSec. Witness protection. More like witness punishment.

The simple solution to keep these guys from killing Darby was to eliminate them first. He couldn't do it. No matter how much he cared for his partner, he couldn't betray everything he and Pike had accomplished. He wouldn't denigrate the man's memory by turning dirty cop. He wanted revenge for Pike, the man who'd lost his life fighting for justice.

The not-so-simple solution was to eliminate the threat to Darby by finding a second witness. A person who knew more about the organization. Or creating someone. Infiltrating their operation would take time. It meant the worst undercover operation of his career. Portraying a dirty DEA agent who was willing to become dirtier.

He'd portray scum again if it meant finding Pike's killer. *And what about you and Darby?* She'd be safe. His wants didn't matter.

He wouldn't be able to protect Darby forever. The government would stash her someplace safe until Thrumburt could file charges. She was their only viable witness. That might be months down the road. The O'Malleys would be secured as well.

He attached photos and sent them to his electronic drop box. Three or four forwards later and no one would be able to trace the source for several days. By then, he'd have the information safely stored in two or three places.

It was even money something had already happened to the original files at the police station. He needed Darby's copies. And he knew how he'd have to get them.

"Dammit!"

"Did you say something?" she asked from behind the closed door.

He'd been so lost in thought he hadn't noticed the water was no longer running. The bathroom door opened and the candlelight made her skin glow. The effect made him want to spout poetry or something as utterly embarrassing. "Just kicked my toe. I hate candlelight."

Liar. He didn't care about the dark, but loved the way the candle glow had turned her hair a deeper auburn. The way the honesty of her heart showed on her face. Her loyalty had reminded him why he'd become a police officer.

Darby had given him back his soul. She'd shown him hers. He knew her.

She wouldn't run. She wouldn't go into witness protection. She wouldn't leave the family she'd just reunited. He knew that much about her.

And as a result, she'd die.

It was that simple.

"You are a very complicated woman with a beautiful heart, Darby O'Malley." He wanted to drag her into his arms but if he did, he wouldn't let go.

"You ain't so bad yourself." She smiled while towel-drying her hair.

A pause stretched into several seconds of silence. He had no freakin' idea where those words had come from and was at a total loss as to what to say next.

"Did you get in touch with Brian?"

"Just getting to the call." He tried to ignore her quizzical look, but gave in with an explanation. "I've been thinking about our next move."

"We decided to hand over the evidence to Thrumburt and find out where Michael was taken."

"Right."

She looked like a woman getting ready for a hot date of country dancing. Low-riding jeans, a green undershirt and a plaid top—layered to make her look ordinary, yet worn specifically to hide her Glock. Anything but ordinary.

"Have you changed your mind about what we should do? Do you think Michael is still in danger?" she asked.

"I'm not worried about your brother." Man, she was cute in tight-fitting jeans. He switched his stare to the phone cards in his hands. "We need to think about your safety."

"Hey, I can take care of myself."

"Right."

She popped his leg with the towel, taking him off guard and causing him to yelp in fake pain.

She giggled. "Seriously, Erren. I'll be fine. I'll testify Monday and we're good. Case closed."

She didn't know the extent of the corruption or how many agencies were involved. No one did. Yet.

All his doubts about what to do next were gone. He'd made up his mind as soon as he'd seen the picture of Knighton, his handler. He'd keep his promise to Pike and the Sergeant Major—protecting Darby at all costs. She had a life and deserved to keep living it. He'd become the witness the government would stash in the middle of nowhere.

He could handle being a nobody stuck in nowheresville in a mindless job, lying to everyone he met. Hadn't he basically done that for the past seven years?

Darby wouldn't last three hours. She just wasn't a liar.

"Guess you should call Thrumburt," she said. "I'm going to dry my hair."

"A message from a dead guy should get their attention," he mumbled too softly to be heard over the hair dryer.

Using Michael's SIM card and subsequently the man's phone number, he selected the attachment to prove he had the evidence, punched in Knighton's number and hit Send. Then opened the phone and switched the SIM cards again. He'd call Thrumburt from the prepay number issued to them at the cabin.

He didn't want to leave her. He fought hard not to pull

Darby into his arms and make love to her one last time. She trusted him enough to make the call with her in the bathroom, but he'd choose his words carefully, just in case she was listening.

"We found it."

"Where should I pick it up?" Thrumburt said.

"The files are electronic. I'll forward to your phone, then give you the whole package when I see you."

"Are they what you expected?"

"Everything we discussed and worse."

"So she's in serious danger." There was no missing the sadness in Thrumburt's voice.

"You could say that."

"When will you turn her over to witness protection?"

"The Medic took O'Malley to the VA on South Lancaster?" Erren answered so Darby could overhear and assume he hadn't known her brother's location earlier. "We'll meet you there within an hour and I'll be proceeding."

"I'll make the arrangements," Thrumburt said. "It's too bad, Erren."

Yeah, it's too bad. A lot of dirty cops would be brought to justice with no guarantee they would go away for life. And with her testimony she'd lose everything. He positioned the phone cards in the green case for safekeeping and stuck it in his pocket.

They'd had a nice run while it had lasted.

The hair dryer cut off and she walked from the bathroom. He plastered a blank look on his face in order to convince Darby their encounter hadn't meant anything to him. He had to become the man who didn't care or she'd see through his act later.

"Let me grab my boots and I'm ready to take off." She walked to the closet. "What did you mean you'll be 'proceeding'?"

Erren dreaded what he had to do next. She wouldn't react

well. He'd hurt her with his stupid remark about wasting his time. They'd worked through it, learning to trust each other. He doubted she'd be able to forgive him for the blindside he was about to hit her with. He was lying *for* her this time in order to protect her family—not because he didn't think she could handle the job. She'd eventually find out, but not before the damage was irreparable.

"I'm dropping you off at the hospital." He inwardly flinched at what he might be losing. It wasn't his. There wasn't any *hope* in his line of business.

"What about the meeting with Brian?" She sat next to him on the bed to pull her boots on and arched her eyebrow.

God, he wanted to kiss her. One last time? Her soft lips begged to be kissed, but he couldn't risk it. If he touched her, he wouldn't be able to hide his desperation and need.

"You can handle the meeting with Thrumburt on your own," he said.

"Where are you going?"

"Hey, my job was to get the package delivered. That'll be done in about half an hour." He forced his words to be normal, unconcerned. The next ones would cut a lot deeper. "All the fun's over here. Time for me to disappear."

Her sharp intake of breath let him know the words had served their purpose. The last thing he wanted was for this afternoon to end. Their oasis in her bedroom was something to keep his nights restless for a long time.

He stood, waiting for her to come back with an equally demeaning phrase.

Call me a coward. Call me a son of a bitch.

She didn't. Her expression froze into a mask. The easy, confident smile had vanished as she'd stiffened. She seemed to be that insecure cop he'd met on her kitchen floor.

He called himself worse and gave her the credit.

"We should probably go." He crossed to the dresser and

slid his gun in the back of his borrowed jeans. He handed her the Glock. "We'll need to collect your backup disks."

He searched her expression in the mirror. Staring at the door, still not speaking. She'd shut down in a way that scared the hell out of him.

Erren had assumed her laptop had been collected after her "kidnapping." But in the hands of the dirty cops, they'd probably confirmed she knew facts which could take them all down. They'd want her eliminated as quickly as possible.

"Not a problem." Her voice was level, without emotion. Those emerald-green eyes held a deep wound he was responsible for. Guilt slashed into him deep and hard...and the scar wouldn't easily go away.

God, he hated hurting her.

She walked into her closet, knelt on the floor and pulled up the carpet. She had a safe. A stack of CDs, a second Glock and some cash were stacked on the floor while she put everything back into place.

Good. A secret she'd kept...even from him.

ONE MINUTE DARBY HAD BEEN a part of an undercover operation, and then with one comment was back to a paper-pushing nonentity. This afternoon she'd found a man who was different—perhaps special. And now she was just a good time.

Thank goodness the drive had been short. Straight highway, deafening engine. Her father's car had provided the perfect reason not to say anything. Now they were parked in front of the VA hospital with the same loud engine idling through the open windows and silence.

What could she say? Or what was she supposed to say? Have a good life? If you're ever in Dallas look me up? Thanks for some of the hottest sex I've ever experienced?

"I'll make sure the Sergeant Major's car is returned," he said.

"Do you need the address?" *Lame*. She really couldn't think of a thing to say.

"I'll find him."

Find her father. Not her. That certainly showed where she rated. She opened the door, and standing by the car, she retrieved the oversized purse where she carried the evidence, money and her Glock.

"Darby?"

She wasn't about to be *lame* again and held her tongue. No telling what she'd end up saying.

"I should have asked about your brother's message as soon as I met you, but I wanted you to…" Secret Agent Man struggled for words. He finally shrugged. "Hell, it was fun."

"All right then. It was…fun." *Be sarcastic, angry—not hurt*. If she said anything else, she might ask him not to go. And that wasn't a good idea. There wasn't anything more to be said or done.

"Just one more thing," he said. "I need your disks."

"What? Why are you asking?"

"I'm not asking, darlin'." His fingernail tapped metal, drawing her attention to the 9mm SIG now in his left hand, resting on his lap. "The bag, hon."

"You're pulling a gun on me? I thought we *trusted* each other." She opened the purse. Why would he want her files? What was he up to? He didn't need the evidence in San Antonio. Would he back off if she pulled her weapon? He wouldn't shoot her. At least she didn't think he would.

"Careful now, O'Malley. I know what you've got in there. And forget the gun in your boot. Woman, your thoughts are as clear as a neon sign flashing on your face."

He laughed and the sound scraped over Darby like fingernails on a chalkboard. He really was a charming SOB. She'd been taken in by everything. She threw a CD case at his chest, wishing she'd aimed a little higher. He didn't flinch, almost as if he'd anticipated she would miss.

"All of them, Darby."

She pulled her backup copies and set them on the floorboard.

"This isn't right, Erren. You know Thrumburt won't have a case without the disks."

"I'll keep them in a safe place."

Could she believe him? What place was safer than the district attorney's office?

"This wasn't a part of the plan."

"Sorry, Darby, but it's always been a part of *my* plan." He reached across the seat and shut the door. "Stay close to your family. We'll get you and your family out of here safely."

The car tires screeched from the parking lot. Fighting back the hot sting of treachery, she also swallowed back the hurtful emotions threatening to explode.

She turned around and walked straight into Brian Thrumburt. "You got here fast."

"As did you, Darby."

"You don't seem too surprised that Agent Rhodes is driving off in my father's car with the copies of my files."

"He warned me that would be a possibility." Thrumburt pushed his glasses up on his nose.

"Don't you want to know where he's headed or go after him or something?"

"Oh, I've got it covered. There's a GPS locator on the cell phone he's using and I have a unit standing by."

A unit? Brian obviously knew more about what was going on than she did. What else was there to do? It seemed they had been lying to her the entire time.

"Are you making arrests tonight?"

"You understand that we can't go into details at the moment." Two men in black suits stepped into the light, showing their U.S. Marshal badges. "Marshals Thomas and Campbell will escort you to a safe house."

"Not until I see my family."

"That's not advisable," he said flatly as if he sincerely believed it was necessary. "They'll be joining you as soon as we secure a location for Michael."

"Listen, Brian, I understand you have to protect your witness from the boogie men. But I'm not going anywhere until I'm assured my family is safe and they know what's going on." She reached out and took hold of her bag. "I'll carry it. The bastard took my gun, but I have stuff for my dad."

He released his grip and she kept her second weapon.

So that was the key to getting away with a lie? Speaking with force? Or speaking like you believed it and in yourself.

"We should check through her purse," said Thomas or Campbell—she hadn't caught who was who.

"Not on your life, buddy." She slung the strap over her shoulder. "I don't let any guy wander through my tampons."

Stay angry. Don't laugh.

The marshal took a step back and gestured toward the hospital's door.

"Keep the car running," Brian instructed.

Thomas or Campbell led the way, the ADA walked next to her and the second marshal stayed outside with the car. Before she could duck into a bathroom and slip the second gun from her boot, they came to a room with an empty chair out front.

Brian knocked. The Medic pulled the door open to a normal-sized hospital room very much like where her brother had been that morning. Michael looked exactly the same. Had it only been fifteen hours since she'd seen him?

Sean stretched in the corner chair. "Hey, Dar."

"How's he doing?" she asked her father as he turned from the window to see her.

"John Doe here," the Sergeant Major nodded toward the Medic, "nicknamed such for his refusal to give his name, says Michael's fine. Everything checks out and his body just needs some uninterrupted rest."

"I actually said the test results in his file were inconclusive and I wasn't certain when or *if* he'd wake up." The Medic directed his opinion to Brian, who obviously wanted an update as well. "Time for my *adiós.*"

The Medic left the room. She hadn't even thanked him.

"Say your goodbyes, Darby. The marshals would like to leave in ten minutes." Brian was the perfect ADA, looking at his watch, addressing the room and not touching his glasses once.

"Everyone can wait outside." Her voice was rigid instead of vibrating like her insides. She hooked her free hand around the strap to keep it from trembling. No one argued or spoke a word. Both men turned on a dime and left. Sean and her dad came closer from the window side of the room and she was finally allowed to see Michael. He looked as if he was in a peaceful sleep and she wanted to shake him, shout him awake like she had when it was her responsibility to make certain he got to school on time.

"What was that dude talking about?" Sean asked, sounding like Michael...but not Michael.

"We found the proof. He hid the information at my house." She stroked Michael's arm, but looked at her family. "He got kicked out of the academy to work undercover, gathering evidence that will put some dirty cops away for a long time."

She wanted to cry and swallowed down the impulse. She was so proud of her little brother. She rubbed his arm again. He'd gotten a tattoo. A symbol they'd used to represent the O'Malley children. An *O* with four points of the compass. Each of them was a different direction, baby brother being west.

"Did you see this, Sean?"

"Cool idea to have a tat of the O'Malley O."

"The guy with glasses said you were leaving with U.S. Marshals?" her father asked. "Are you in trouble for this morning?"

"Weird thing about that evidence, Dad, is I'm part of what Michael was protecting. I can corroborate the information and I need to testify."

I've made two promises I won't break—to keep you safe and to put the bastard who shot Pike away. Erren's words pounded her brain.

"Are you going into witness protection?" Sean asked.

"Only for a while."

"Are you sure? If they've already killed one police officer, shot Michael and tried to kill you... What's to stop them from trying again?" Her brother's voice began to rise. "Do you know who did this?"

Oh, my God!

"That mule-headed chameleon." She waved Brian inside the door and poked him in the chest. "Where has he gone?"

"Excuse me?" Brian looked around the room for help, falling back another step as she poked his chest again.

Sean and her father stood with their arms crossed and lips firmly closed, silently backing her every move.

"Erren wouldn't have driven away from unfinished business. Even with the evidence Michael collected, we don't know who pulled the trigger. He didn't leave town. He's gone to confront those monsters on his own." She would do whatever was necessary to save her partner from himself. "And you're letting him."

"It's our best course of action." Brian couldn't retreat any farther with his back to the wall and Darby's finger in his chest.

"I want to know where Erren is headed and what you two planned while I was out of the room at the cabin."

"That's on a need-to-know basis."

"Oh, I definitely need to know and you sure as hell are about to tell me."

"You can't threaten me, Darby."

"If there's one thing I know about my daughter, son, it's that she doesn't make threats." Her father widened his stance and placed his hands on his hips. "She keeps promises."

Chapter Fifteen

"Brian, tell me where he's going." Darby stood nose-to-nose with the attorney. She hadn't screamed and didn't need to fake anything. She sounded and felt desperate.

Whatever Erren said he was doing, his real intention was to find Pike's murderer. None of the evidence they had secured told them who had pulled the trigger. She knew firsthand that putting that slimeball on the fast track to state prison was the only thing that was important to Agent Rhodes.

Definitely more important than she was to him.

"We need to get you to a safe house as soon as possible." Brian still stood next to the wall. The confidence in his tone was slipping. "It's imperative that you receive protection."

"I don't think you recognize my daughter's look. You may as well give in. She's going to get her way." The Sergeant Major's stance may have seemed intimidating to an assistant district attorney, but to her he'd never appeared more caring.

"Erren said he was forwarding the pictures to you. Are they on your BlackBerry?" She held her hand out, expecting him to hand over the phone.

"We don't have time for you to hunt for clues," Brian said. He looked at her family. "This is highly inappropriate. We'll go over everything at the safe house."

"I don't have time to waste," she told him, motioning for

the phone. She restrained her foot from tapping impatiently as Brian didn't react.

Her brother took two threatening steps toward Brian, who yanked the phone from his pocket. "The longer we stay here, the more you're putting your family at risk."

Darby took the phone and moved to the chair in the corner, skimming through the pictures slowly, studying details she hadn't noticed with Erren next to her.

This is what Erren had been doing when she'd finished her shower. They'd seen the same pictures. What had he seen to change his mind? He'd been loving and caring then had become withdrawn…even for him. Scrolling through the evidence sheets shouldn't have meant anything to him. What had she missed? So what did he see? Someone he knew?

Whatever it had been, it was enough to send her straight to a safe house.

"Time's up, Darby." Stepping forward, Brian reached for his phone.

Her brother put a hand out to stop him. "She's done when she's done, Mr. Thrumburt."

Each picture was important or Michael wouldn't have included it. She focused on the small details. Trying to connect the dots. She was determined to discover what Erren had seen that had changed his mind. What was his urgency that caused him to shift plans?

This won't be over until I find Pike's murderer. How many times had Erren said this to her?

Maybe it wasn't what Erren had seen, but what he hadn't.

"He's after Pike's murderer." She looked at Brian for confirmation. "Erren is out for revenge."

"We don't know who pulled the trigger, but these men are responsible."

Brian gestured to the phone. "Rhodes accepted that we

wouldn't know what truly happened that night until your brother awakens."

"Is that what he told you? He's a very good liar."

Good enough to convince you to walk away.

"We really must leave, Darby." He turned toward her father, perhaps to make a plea. The motion pulled his left sleeve higher on his wrist, exposing more of the ink stain she'd seen the day before.

The ink smeared on the back of his wrist wasn't an accident. It was a faded dragon's tail—or a tattoo the ADA was having removed. A very sketchy, not well-done yet completely recognizable gang sign. She flipped through the pictures and found the young woman who looked totally wasted. A hand helped her shoot more drugs into her arm. A hand with a dragon…

Brian's hand. He constantly pulled at his sleeves, constantly covered his hands. He'd been playing them this entire time. It explained why the men involved knew to look through Pike's picture albums and her box of photos.

Thrumburt was dirty.

Erren! He was walking into a trap.

Control your breathing. Don't let Thrumburt know you figured it out. Set your emotions aside, O'Malley, she could hear Erren's voice whispering in her ear.

Okay, think. Erren probably had a plan, but he'd sent her to Thrumburt, so he didn't know he was dirty. Her partner didn't have all the facts and she was the only person who could warn him he was in danger.

But Thrumburt had called the U.S. Marshals to arrange for her protection. It didn't make sense. She stared at the phone, unwilling to risk anyone seeing her face. She had to get herself under control and think like a cop, act like Erren. She could play the role of an undercover agent. It was about more than lying.

Obviously, Erren hadn't shared all of his plans. What if the marshals' arrival had taken Thrumburt by surprise? What if the Medic had called them here to take his place? There were more possibilities than she had time to consider.

Thrumburt didn't act as if he knew she could identify him in the pictures. His easiest route was to blame everything on Erren. If she deleted the picture it may buy Erren more time. She'd get Thrumburt away from her family, ditch the marshals and find her partner.

Piece of cake.

"It's no use. I'll never discover what Rhodes saw or how his mind works." If she couldn't lie, then she'd tell the truth. "He has a compulsion to find Pike's killer that I don't understand."

"Let him do his job, Darby." Thrumburt took his phone from her. "He knows what he's doing."

"I know he's capable." She looked at the floor. If she looked at Brian, she was certain he'd see through her. "Give us a minute, will you? Then I'll be ready to go."

The dirty ADA left the room. She hurried to her father, digging in her purse for the Glock.

"I guess Rhodes is Paladin?" he asked.

"Yes, sir. If you've ever trusted me, Dad, do it now." She hugged him, pressing the gun into his hand. "I don't have time to explain. Do whatever it takes to protect Michael. You've got to get out of here and hide."

"Then you need to come with us," her brother said, matching her whisper.

"I can't." She wasn't going to break apart. Not now. She swallowed the emotion building in her throat and hugged her dad one last time, pulling Sean into the group for a quick squeeze. "He saved my life and Michael's. He doesn't know he's walking into an ambush."

"Let me come," Sean said.

"There's no way you can go alone," her father said at the same time.

With a hand on each of their shoulders, she looked between them, tilting her head toward her little brother. "It's going to take you both to get him out of here and protect him. It's my responsibility to warn my partner."

And the only way to ensure you're all safe. Time for this woman to come to the rescue.

"I don't like this, Dar." Sean's voice sounded angry, with more emotion than she'd heard from him since he was a kid.

"You know I can take care of myself."

"At least take the Glock." Her father pushed it back toward her.

"Come on, Dad. I've got another in my boot and extra clips in my purse. I'm a cop, remember?"

"But also my little girl."

"You taught us to never leave a man behind," she whispered. "Erren's my man, Dad."

"Keep your head down, shoot straight, and we'll see you Sunday for the Cowboys game."

"Yes, sir." Another quick hug. "I've got to go. Take care of him."

Brian was watching for her through the little window in the door and pushed it open. The marshal walked into the room after she'd left.

"He's staying behind." Thrumburt placed his hand in the small of her back to guide her down the hall. "I think you're right, Darby. We need to find Erren. We're the only people he can trust."

The man's hand wasn't warm like Erren's. It didn't comfort her in any way. It creeped her out and it took all of her control to keep from cringing.

"Why the change of heart?" she asked.

"Erren's GPS indicates a location in Dallas. He's not headed back to San Antonio like we thought. I've already got a unit moving into position to back him up, but I believe I should be there to make certain things go smoothly. We wouldn't want the cops to shoot him on sight."

Or you want to be there to ensure that's exactly what happens.

They climbed into the waiting car driven by the second marshal. Thrumburt sat in front. She took the back. The sedan was dark inside as they pulled away from the hospital, but not dark enough to cover her movements. Getting to her second Glock wouldn't be an easy task.

"Where's Thomas?" their driver asked.

"Change of plans," Thrumburt announced. "You have the GPS location where Rhodes went. Take us there."

"My job's to get O'Malley to a safe house, not follow a rogue agent into the seedy part of Dallas."

"Your job is to do what you're told." Thrumburt raised his voice and his speech became less refined and precise.

Darby watched the exchange. Thrumburt had never lost his cool—he played the intimidated dork to perfection. So...

He knows. Somehow. She'd messed up again by deleting the picture. Of course, he'd already seen himself in it and he would notice it was gone.

"Campbell," she said, catching his eye in the mirror. With a frightened expression, she shook her head and pointed to Thrumburt.

Campbell slowly reached in his jacket, but the ADA pulled a gun. The marshal slowly replaced his hand on the steering wheel.

"Keep driving. Just get us to that location." He kept the gun pointed at Campbell. "Nice try, Darby. Gently lift your purse over the seat to me."

She did as he commanded. "What now, Brian? How are you going to cover this up?"

"Rhodes has taken care of that for me. It couldn't be better if I'd planned it myself."

"That was a stellar performance at the safe house. You really had me fooled. All your faked emotion, I would give you a round of applause if you didn't disgust me." He was responsible for her friend's death and she wanted to tear the man limb from limb. "You put Michael in a coma and killed Pike, you little bastard."

"You killed a cop?" Campbell chimed in, hands gripping the steering wheel tighter.

"You," Brian said to the marshal, "should keep your mouth shut and take us in exactly the direction that little arrow on the screen is pointing."

"We should be there in about ten minutes."

Brian thrust his fist into the side of the marshal's head. The car swerved out of their lane and quickly back in, resulting in surrounding horns and her loss of breath.

"I said no talking. Just drive."

"You are a bastard of the first order," she said.

"Darby, Darby, Darby." Thrumburt shook his head as if he couldn't understand why she was disgusted. "I didn't pull the trigger, but I suppose you could give me credit for eliminating the threats to my operation."

"Are you seriously going to compare yourself to a businessman? You're a crook. A drug dealer. You're responsible for several deaths and you'll pay with your own life."

"That's a debt I'll never pay, sweetheart."

She could see the GPS arrow getting closer to her partner's location. She didn't know what to do. Whatever Erren was planning, these men were several steps ahead and confident their cover-up would succeed.

The only way it would work was if they were all dead.

Dead DEA agent, dead U.S. Marshal, dead Dallas cop. How in the world would they pull something like that off?

Campbell's questioning eyes met hers in the mirror. He pointed to the GPS and raised his finger like a gun. She understood. They had to do something before they reached their destination.

"Stop here." Thrumburt opened his phone and sent a text. Within seconds he received a reply. "We'll be meeting them at a more private location. Straight for three blocks and take a left at the stop sign."

They pulled into a parking lot of an old warehouse building in South Dallas. They were running out of time. She made eye contact in the mirror with Campbell again, who cut his eyes toward the gun still pointing in his side.

Thrumburt wasn't wearing his seat belt. Could Campbell speed up and slam the ADA's head into the dashboard before the airbag exploded? The marshal's arms stiffened on the wheel. Using slow, controlled movements, she pulled the middle seat belt across her lap and snapped it shut.

"Don't get any heroic ideas, Campbell," Thrumburt said.

The marshal punched the gas, heading toward the side of the building.

Darby braced herself for the impact.

"Stop!" their captor screamed.

She should cover her head and duck to the floor, but she couldn't move. She was frozen by the barrel of the .45 yo-yoing between her and the marshal. The side of the building grew larger in the front windshield.

She had to be prepared to take the gun from Thrumburt. Her hand was on her seat belt, ready to pull it open.

The crash jolted her body as the scream of the gun pierced her ears.

Chapter Sixteen

Another frickin' dark alley. Another setup. Another double cross.

Erren drove past the meeting point, searching from the car for a possible ambush. Nothing in sight, but plenty of places for one to happen. The alley could have been a duplicate of where he'd met Beavis and Butthead. And Knighton, his not-so-trustworthy handler, had indisputable knowledge of first-rate betrayals.

Time to end this.

He parked half a block away, keeping the Sergeant Major's car out of the line of fire. It was the least he could do for Darby's family. If all went as planned he'd pick up the Cougar and return it soon. He walked back to the meet, prepared to follow through for Pike—no matter the outcome.

He caught sight of the men lurking at the edge of the shadows and lifted his hands in the air. Two were behind him with guns at his back before he made it twenty feet into the alley. Whoever was behind this operation wasn't taking a chance this time. The men pushed him between his shoulders, tripping him up, making it difficult to walk into the darkness—much more thorough than Beavis and Butthead.

One man he recognized from Darby's house. It was the cop who'd shot at them, now walking with a limp. He wasn't gentle about searching Erren for weapons or a wire. "He's clean."

Erren watched a tall form walk into the low light of the alley.

"Well, well, well, if it ain't Agent Rhodes," said a familiar voice, confirming his suspicions.

"Knighton," he acknowledged.

Erren's long-term portrayal of the San Antonio drug dealer came easily to his mind and actions. He purposefully changed the way he stood, talked and didn't meet the DEA handler's eyes. Then an image of sitting across Darby's legs jumped into his head.

Fantastic. She's going to get me killed and she isn't even here.

"How's the leg?" he asked the cop limping by him.

"As far as the legit cops are concerned," he answered, "you kidnapped one of Dallas's finest at gunpoint. We could shoot now and never ask questions."

Knighton circled him. He hadn't been surprised to see him. They'd been waiting to take care of the problem. No curiosity about what Erren had to offer. They didn't act anxious or apprehensive. Damn.

Made sense to have cops pointing the weapons. Limpy Cop had Erren's cell and tossed it to the DEA handler.

"Did you wonder why a dead guy called?" Erren asked.

"Naw. Not a problem. You brought the evidence to me and we'll get rid of the problem child and his sister later." He took a step toward Erren and hit him hard in the chest.

The force of Knighton's fist caused Erren to move backwards. The filthy scumbag turned his back and Erren balled his fingers into fists to stop himself from retaliating. "So you figured out O'Malley's not dead yet. Okay. But you still might have a problem."

Knighton turned on a dime and Erren couldn't avoid the

backhand that came along with it. He didn't fake the pained moan that escaped before he had control. The staggering blow was meant to knock him to his knees, but he managed to stay on his feet.

"My problem will end when I get rid of you."

"Like I came here, unarmed, with my only bargaining chip on a cell phone?" Erren shook his head and pointed his thumb to his bruising chest area. "Not dumb, man."

He hoped he was driving Knighton nuts. Erren needed him angry and thinking unclearly. He wanted answers.

"*If* you emailed the pictures somewhere. *If* you got someone to believe you. *If* you could make all that happen in an hour. A lot of ifs for a washed-up undercover with no handler and no police academy babysitter." He looked at Cop Number Two on his left. "Get rid of him."

The cop took Erren's arm, giving a tug to begin walking.

"Did I mention that I have to check my drop-box account once an hour or it forwards to the Feds?"

Erren allowed himself to grin at Knighton's volatile reaction. At this point, any emotion the man showed gave Erren information.

"Do you really expect me to believe that TV babble? This isn't playacting, but I am curious. Where did you find O'Malley's phone? It wasn't on him at the hospital."

"You missed it at his sister's place."

"That's what I get for sending idiots." Knighton looked at Cop Number Two.

Erren shrugged.

"Why are you here? What did you hope to gain besides getting killed?" Knighton finally asked.

Erren yanked his arm free from Cop Number Two. "Now that you mention it, I'm here to deal. I want a cut of the action."

"There's nothing you have that I want."

"Just a bigger distribution area. I've got San Antonio and south Texas connections that will increase your profits." Erren crossed his arms, trying to remain confident in spite of the growing suspicion he was in over his head.

"Not if you're taking a piece of the pie." Knighton stepped closer and threw a right punch into Erren's gut.

It took several seconds to catch his breath. "You're really not playing nice."

"We're not playin' at all. I want to know where the pictures are stored and where you stashed O'Malley's files."

Son of a bitch... One person knew he had the files. That little weasel Thrumburt. He'd sent Darby straight to the U.S. Marshals. Darby was safe and away from this scum.

"The files are safe," he forced out. He'd hated to use his favor at the FBI, but he'd called as soon as he'd pulled away from the VA hospital. The files were extremely safe.

Knighton took the opportunity to punch him in the gut again, dropping him to his knees.

"Put him in the van," Knighton ordered the cops. "This place is too public for what we need to do."

Each cop took him under an arm and dragged him across the broken asphalt to the end of the alley. They tossed him in the back of an empty panel van. Cop Number Two zip-tied his wrists, riding in the back with him. Knighton drove and hit every pothole possible.

This was definitely not the plan.

The ride was too noisy to hear anything said up front but the glow of a cell phone reflected on the windshield. At least the ride was short and he didn't have to roll around too long. When the van slowed to a stop, he pushed himself to a sitting position and waited for the door to open.

Staying was risky, but it was too early to escape. He would always find a way out. This time he wouldn't leave until he discovered who pulled the trigger of that .38 caliber.

The two cops started to drag him again and he shrugged them off. "I got this, guys."

They moved inside an abandoned warehouse. Dust floated in the low-lit corner where they were headed. The smell of dirt and gas was strong, making it harder to breathe. He tried to focus on the far dark region and thought he saw a car. Lots of doors and hiding places. Looking up, he caught the bottom view of multiple catwalks running the length of the building.

Eyes front. Just thinking about being that high off the ground made his knees turn to Jell-O and knots form in his stomach.

"Want to explain again why you're so valuable to us?" Knighton asked.

"You want the files. Right now, I'm thinking they're the only things keeping me standing upright instead of in a shallow grave somewhere."

"You think we need you, Rhodes? We've been dishing this up in major cities for three years. We don't need nothin' from you."

"Except the files." He lifted his head, catching Knighton's look of frustration. Erren stood as straight as he could manage with his abdomen cramping. "If I join you, O'Malley's copies of the evidence sheets never surface."

"Come on in," Knighton called into the dark, then faced Erren. "So you think you have us in a hard spot?"

What the hell was going on?

"What are you talking about? All I want is a slice of the action."

"That's not what you're gonna get," Limpy Cop said.

Thrumburt stepped into the circle of light, a little worse for wear. His forehead was bleeding and there was a layer of dust on his suit. Erren could imagine getting the turncoat in a headlock and snapping his skinny neck. But he wouldn't.

Who pulled the trigger? Just tell me who pulled the trigger?

One answer and this whole thing would be over.

"So the little man turns out to be the big boss man," Erren said.

Thrumburt kept the smug look and didn't react to being called the boss man. Knighton didn't react either. Each had a triumphant stare, declaring himself the winner. How? Erren had the evidence that would put them all away for years.

What did they have?

"Bring her in," Knighton said. "Now we'll see if you're still so cocky."

Darby? She was the only person in his life they could use as leverage.

The Medic should have called the U.S. Marshals' office to protect the O'Malleys. How had she gotten away from the hospital?

She came into the circle of light, her face and neck smeared with blood, her hands bound in front of her. Erren's moment of panic must have shown in his eyes. She immediately shook her head. "I'm okay. It's not mine."

God, then who? Had Thrumburt killed her family?

"They're going to kill us no matter what you do, Erren." She looked at her feet, reminding him about the gun in her boot.

Nice job!

"That's enough!" Thrumburt yelled. Then he turned to Cop Number Two. "Shut her up."

"He shot and killed a U.S. Marsh—"

The cop slapped her then cupped his hand over her mouth. At least he hadn't knocked her unconscious. Darby's presence changed everything.

Time to take control.

"Anyone know what time it is?" he asked. Four pairs of eyes indicated he'd totally lost his mind. "I'm just asking, 'cause the Feds are expecting a phone call and I wouldn't want them to worry."

"What? You said you had to contact the drop box to *keep* the Feds from getting the evidence," Knighton yelled.

Erren shrugged and took great pleasure in saying, "I lied."

Chapter Seventeen

Was Erren lying about having called the Feds? Did he really expect someone to burst through the doors?

Standing in a condemned warehouse, hands bound, covered in blood spatter, she wasn't going to stop and think about it too much. She watched for any sign—an indication that Erren was going to break away or if he really expected some branch of the federal government to save their hides.

More than once she looked at her right boot, hoping that he remembered she'd dropped her Glock inside.

"Do it, Knighton. Have some fun," Thrumburt told the tall man. "See how much he'll spout off watching us slice up his girlfriend."

Fear took hold of her legs. She wanted to run. Thrumburt was a cold-blooded killer. He'd easily pulled the trigger on Campbell just before the crash. She had no doubts he'd do anything to her to obtain the information he wanted.

"What time is it?" Erren asked. Dropping his gaze to her feet. He was stalling. He knew about her weapon. "I just need to know one thing. Which of you dirtbags shot Walter Pike?"

After his smile and laughter, maybe it was the shock of hearing the vehement, hate-filled syllables of the last question that silenced the men. But it didn't stop them all from looking to the tall man Thrumburt had called Knighton, who stood with a smug look of satisfaction, a grin growing on his face.

Erren had his answer.

While the men had all eyes glued to Knighton waiting for his reaction, Erren dove across the pool of light. His body rolled several times before reaching her feet. She dropped to the ground sending her legs in his direction. He tugged and her right boot slipped off, dumping the 9mm onto the dusty floor.

The men scrambled for cover, shooting blindly. Darby rolled to her knees ready to head toward the exit. She ducked at the gunfire. At least three locations.

"Don't kill him yet," Thrumburt shouted. "Idiots, we need the evidence."

"If you're okay," Erren yelled, "can you get that cute little behind of yours in gear?"

She leaped up and darted toward the car, stopping for cover behind a pillar. Erren stopped with her and pinned her back to the concrete, covering her, his hands—and gun—above his head. He couldn't get a shot off that way, but their bodies were completely connected.

"God, what were you thinking?" His eyes searched her face, landing on her lips. "Did you come to rescue me?"

"I followed my partner, who took off totally on his own."

He was happy. She recognized the lightheartedness in his undisguised voice. The real Erren had his body pressed into hers. He was the only man she could think of who might be ignoring the rain of deadly gunfire to hold her.

His lips captured hers in a short but hungry kiss.

"Is the cavalry really coming or—"

"They're coming. But not for at least—" he leaned back and brought her wrists closer to read the time on her watch "—ten minutes."

"So you aren't stupid after all?"

Gunfire sounded around them, getting a bit too close for comfort.

"You know we have to make a run for it." He smiled at her as if they did this every day. Maybe he did. "I'll lay down cover. Go."

She heard the bullets zing past her ears as she ran to the car for the extra ammunition in her purse. She made it to the far side of the wrecked sedan and yanked open the passenger door. Ignoring the dead marshal in the front seat, she grabbed the clips and tried to hand them to her partner.

But Erren wasn't behind her.

As DARBY RAN TO SAFETY, Erren caught movement to his left and watched Thrumburt racing up the stairs by the far wall.

The second-story offices would give the son of a bitch the perfect shot to take her out at the car. He saw the old metal catwalks for the warehouse and his gut clenched.

"Dammit. You just had to go up," he muttered.

Brian had ordered Pike's death, even if Knighton had pulled the trigger. Neither one was going to escape and neither would harm another person he loved.

Loved? It was a hell of a time to come to the realization that he loved Darby. A fast-and-furious relationship so far, but one he could envision lasting a lifetime. "Guess there's a first time for everything."

Zigzagging to the enclosed staircase, he wished he had a knife to cut through the plastic around his wrists. His eyes adjusted to the dim light as he climbed, each step harder than the last. The dizziness made his head swim. He didn't know where the others had hidden or if they were waiting to ambush them. At the top of the stairs he could see Thrumburt ten feet away with a .45 pointed toward Darby.

The solidness under his feet was gone and the only thing left was the warehouse floor far beneath him. He knew there was a metal walkway beneath his feet, but the look down sent his equilibrium seesawing. He had to do this. The bastard was about to shoot the woman he loved. He couldn't fail Darby. He ignored the openness of the warehouse and concentrated on the solid wall to his right so he could run.

Erren aimed. Fired. Missed.

His hands shook from the vertigo. He'd never hit his target. The shot alerted Thrumburt, who jerked to attention and pulled the trigger.

"No!" Erren screamed, and ran and threw himself at Thrumburt.

They crashed to the metal grate. Erren backhanded the smaller man, but with his hands bound, he was at a disadvantage. He grabbed Thrumburt's gun hand and knocked it against the grate until the gun fell to the floor below.

Thrumburt punched and kicked, fighting like a boy who was scrambling for his life. With limited hand movement, Erren used his knee and pressed it into the turncoat's abdomen.

He controlled one of Pike's killers but he needed to find Darby. Had she been shot or made it out of the building? He looked down, trying to find her.

The view through the metal grate narrowed into a diamond pattern closing in on itself. The room spun. He closed his eyes to block the vertigo and nausea.

"Erren!" He heard Darby's voice just below him. "I'm coming up."

Thank God, she was alive.

Thrumburt thrust his body upward and Erren flew forward, his stomach hitting the rail. His knees locked and he couldn't move. He slammed his eyes shut again and froze.

"OPEN YOUR EYES, COWBOY. I sort of need your help down here." Darby clung to the edge of the grate, but didn't have the strength in her arms to pull herself back to the walkway.

Erren was frozen on the handrail several feet from her. He pulled himself backward until he was off the rail and flush against the wall.

"Come on, look at me. I'm hanging by a thread, cowboy." Dangling in the air, she was a sitting duck for a spare bullet.

Erren's eyes opened, searching for her voice until his gaze locked with hers. Her Knight Errant fell to his stomach and scooted forward—bound hands in front of him—to hang slightly over the edge until he caught her closest forearm.

"If I had more than *one* hand..." He stared into her eyes, never looking away. "This would be a lot easier."

Sweat beaded on his brow and dropped to her shoulder. His strength amazed her as he lifted her up. She locked her fingers around his wrist and swung her free hand on top of the grate walkway. She could hear Thrumburt below them, sifting through debris for his .45.

"Darby, we're almost there. Pull, darlin'." Erren's voice was steady, unlike his arms, which shook with the strain. He lifted, she pulled with her free hand and within seconds she was on the catwalk beside him.

"No time to wait around. Thrumburt's looking for his weapon and I don't know where the others have gone," she informed him, cupping his chin with her hands. "Focus straight ahead and let's get the hell out of here."

"I'm fine," he said, pulling at the plastic around his wrists. "Just how did you cut the zip-ties?"

"Oh." She pulled an all-utility knife from her pocket and cut him free. "I always carry one in my purse. Left it in the car." She pulled a full clip from her back pocket. "Along with a change of ammo."

"We have some bad guys to catch."

She stood first and retrieved the Glock from the grate, and he followed, a hair of a second behind her.

"Why haven't they left?" she asked.

"They can't. Not as long as we're alive." He brought her close to him and she drew on his strength.

"That was a bit too close for comfort," he said softly into her neck. "Try not to fall off any balconies again."

"Or be pushed by running attorneys."

"I was wondering how you got down there." Still holding her back to his chest, he touched his forehead to her shoulder. "We're going to make a break for it."

"Liar. You want me to leave so you can shoot it out with Pike's murderers."

He smiled. "Can't blame a guy for trying to save his gal."

His gal? She could live with that.

She gave him a quick kiss. "Once a day is more than enough. Thank you very much."

"Keep the gun and hand over the knife."

She did as instructed. "What's the plan?"

"Not certain what they're going to do, but it'll happen fast. They've had a lot of time to regroup. Stay close." He cupped her shoulders. "We go together, partner."

"Looks like your Fed buddies forgot about you, Rhodes," Thrumburt yelled from below the catwalk.

"I want to be clear," he said.

"Yeah?" she asked.

"Might as well give up, Rhodes. You won't get out of here alive," Knighton shouted from their left.

"We're getting out. We're only three blocks from major traffic," she said.

He shook his head. "Wishful thinking, Darby."

"Or we can wait it out upstairs in one of the offices." His

formidable look confirmed their situation was more dire than she wanted to admit. "Then what do we do?"

"The truth?" He still held her by her shoulders. "Shoot to kill, Darby. Don't be soft with these guys. Their only intention is to kill you."

The last moments in the car replayed in her mind—Thrumburt raising the gun and shooting Campbell in the head. Erren was right. Until all the witnesses were dead, these men would be a danger to her, her family and Erren.

"They're trying to kill us. It's not the time to debate obtaining witnesses," she said. "I've got your back."

"I know." Erren squeezed her shoulders and stepped around the surprise of his life. Should he tell her? Did she already know? He loved looking into her emerald eyes. Even in the low light of the warehouse he could see the green sparks, the life, the fun.

They'd need lots of luck to walk away from this mess he'd gotten them into. *Then* they'd talk—possibly including a future.

Time to go.

"Thrumburt's on our right," he explained. "Knighton's to the left, the other two cops are probably placed to catch us in a cross fire. Can you take out the light?" She nodded. "This is going to happen fast so stay low and run like the place is on fire until you're out of the building. And Darby?"

"Yes?"

"Stay alive for me, will ya?"

"Right back atcha, cowboy."

No weapon—except for the knife—meant there was no way to cover Darby as he waited for her to swing around the door, shoot out the light and run. Which she did to perfection. Two shots hit their mark and shoved the warehouse into complete darkness. Cracks of light broke through every twenty or so feet. He couldn't see much, but that meant Thrumburt and his men couldn't see anything either.

Erren tapped Darby's shoulder, causing her to halt. He'd said to run, but they couldn't. They needed to determine where Limpy and Second Cop were. They could be waiting for them just outside. The results wouldn't be nice.

He took the lead along the wall, waiting to hear any movement. Nothing. Just the rusty swinging of that hanging light Darby had hit.

His partner backed into him. They'd learned to work well together. He could trust her—something he hadn't done in a long time.

It was an old trick, but he picked up a small cylinder from the floor, motioned to Darby what he was going to do, and threw it to the opposite side of the room. They ducked to their knees, hearing and seeing where two of the men were located as they fired at the sound.

Whether officer or daughter of an U.S. Army sergeant major, Darby responded by returning rapid fire in the direction of the first shooter. He heard the sound of a body crumbling onto the debris and quickly joined Darby on the floor, rolling away from her to avoid someone taking them out the same way.

He'd been right to assume she'd be a good shot and had a feeling her father had a hand in that accomplishment.

Then all hell broke loose. He rolled directly into Knighton, who was much closer than he'd considered. The tall man fell and they struggled. Erren lost his grip on the knife. Knighton landed a strong punch to Erren's wounded side.

"You're…done…man," he said, trying to let Darby know his position.

Knighton turned the weapon into Erren's chest. Erren grabbed and shoved back. And just like in any good movie, the gun went off. Knighton collapsed on Erren's chest.

In his split-second acknowledgment that Knighton had shot himself, Erren heard a struggle back toward the area where Darby had hung from the catwalk. "Darby? Answer me!"

Something crashed. Erren ran toward the sound.

"The little bastard...is stronger," she yelled, "than he looks."

They rolled into the moonlight. Before he could reach them, Thrumburt landed a punch to the side of Darby's head. Erren's mind turned into a mad, bizarre place of protectiveness he'd never experienced. He threw himself at Thrumburt, shoving him off Darby and landing in the dark. Thrumburt might have been a match for his partner, but the ADA didn't stand a chance against Erren's wrath.

He had Thrumburt pinned to the ground and could feel Brian's flesh giving way with each pounding of his fist before Darby stopped his arm.

"He's out cold, Erren."

He caught his breath and looked her over from head to toe. "You're okay?"

"I'll probably have a headache for three days, but I'm fine."

He heard the distinct noise of a hammer being pulled back. "Watch out!"

Leaning into Darby's legs, he pulled her to the ground and caught her on his chest just as a lone shot was fired.

It hit Thrumburt instead. Darby turned and fired toward the catwalk. They heard a body drop to the metal, then thud to the floor somewhere in front of them, a .38-caliber revolver in the hand of Second Cop.

"You are really good with that thing," Erren said.

"I had three brothers for competition. Where's the other guy who wrecked my house?"

They listened for any movement, heard the van's engine start up and heard sirens getting closer.

"Doesn't sound like Limpy's around any longer. Almost over," he told her. "You're safe."

"So are you," she said with a saucy tone, as if she'd done her fair share of the work. She was right. She'd saved him in more ways than one.

THE FBI AGENT ERREN HAD called to clean up this cross-agency betrayal stood at the door of the warehouse—staying out of the "cleanup." Erren had risked everything to turn the evidence over to the FBI. It was one long shot he'd played and actually won. Agent Steve Woods gestured for Erren to join him. A single head nod meant it was time to leave.

But once Erren left, he wasn't certain when he'd get back to Darby. She didn't know he had to leave and she'd be madder than a hornet when he couldn't be reached.

But that's what happened. There couldn't be a record of his involvement. He'd give a statement. He'd testify if necessary. But he couldn't be seen by the numerous officers filling the warehouse. He couldn't be photographed by the media, who would soon be on the scene after discovering an ADA and a police officer had been killed. He had to disappear.

Officer O'Malley would be the hero of the day. Spitting mad, but a hero. The glory of bringing down a major crime ring would be forced upon her to face alone—at least until her brother woke up from his coma.

She was phenomenal. If things had been different they might have gotten together. He shook the impossible dream from his mind. This was it. He had to say goodbye. He just couldn't figure out how.

Joining her at the bottom of the stairs, he ignored the FBI and said, "They picked up Limpy Cop."

"I'd love to read your reports one day—Beavis, Butthead, Limpy Cop. What's your nickname for me?"

"Amazing." He sidestepped making a fool of himself and

changed the subject. "By the way, thanks for coming to my rescue."

"Some rescue. I thought you'd be very, *very* angry I screwed up the entire operation."

"Woman, you've got to work on your self-esteem. You saved me. Big time." He shook his head, smiling—and liking that he didn't have to calculate how to smile anymore. "Remember when I said to trust me, Darby?"

"Yeah, but who is it that I'm really trusting?" She arched that sexy eyebrow toward her forehead.

He tugged her into the circle of his arms and kissed her deep and much too short of a time. "Just a regular guy. Remember that, hon."

She pushed back on his chest and lightly tapped his unbruised cheek. "No problem."

He pulled her more tightly into his arms, not wanting her to leave. Taking an extra minute for one last goodbye kiss. When they broke apart, he still held on to her hand.

"You were awesome through this whole operation, Darby. Pike would have been proud. I had the right O'Malley all along."

She smiled, nodded in the direction of the police officers calling to her and walked away.

He watched her go speak with the officers documenting the bust, the shots and evidence. The FBI agent waved to him again. It was time to leave Darby and disappear.

This is what he did. This was his life.

But it didn't have to be…not any longer.

Chapter Eighteen

Darby sat at her academy desk working hard. Paper pushing. Brainless work that ironically allowed her mind to overthink everything.

There had been no contact or record of Erren Rhodes and she'd been forced to lie, accepting unsolicited congratulations each time she'd stepped out of her office. Her partner had been right about her—she hated the lies. She avoided as many fellow officers as she could. She'd been forced to take credit for the drug bust. So she stayed in her office.

Three weeks and Pike's desk was still empty. He'd been credited for helping her and dying in the line of duty, when no one would have been caught without *his* investigation. The P.D. wanted the credit for the bust to save face with the community. Good cops put away bad cops.

So was Erren a bad cop only out for revenge? Or had everything between them been about the job? Had he been playing a role all along? Erren said to trust him. The real question was could she trust her instincts and just move on?

Today would be a good day to begin. She looked at the new clock, housed in a chunk of amber, sitting on her desk. "Pike's replacement is already ten minutes late."

She had the duty of showing him the ropes, introducing him around the department and taking him to lunch. All a direct order from her captain. Definitely something she didn't want to do. There would be more lies and congratulations she didn't deserve.

Erren had been right. Lying wasn't her style, even though she'd become quite good at it to protect his cover.

She fingered the new amber paperweight sitting on the corner of her desk. She leaned forward and dropped her head into her hands. *Get a grip, girl. You didn't really know him. It was just a tense situation and you can't expect him to feel close to you.*

First thing was to get rid of some of this amber. She shoved the amber gel pen and the amber-colored worry stones into her top drawer. A terrific-looking amber-colored sweater hung in her closet at home. Not to mention the shade of dark amber she'd painted her bedroom or the new set of amber-tinted glasses she had in the kitchen—still sitting on the counter, wrapped in their plastic sack with the receipt inside ready to return.

Amber.

The glasses were the last straw. On the way home from the mall she'd realized her new favorite color was the same shade Erren's eyes turned in passion. She'd known her Secret Agent Man for a few days, he'd disappeared and she'd missed him every minute since. She was so hopelessly over the top with feelings for the man.

It had been almost three weeks and she hadn't received a single word from Erren. Her father's car was left only a few blocks from the warehouse and had been found easily enough. Darby the cop understood her part in aiding in his disappearance. But Darby the woman remembered the way he'd looked at her when their lives had been in danger... Well, she had thought—and hoped—that he'd at least contact *her*.

Nothing was needed from Erren Rhodes to wrap up the case awaiting prosecution. Her statement had been taken by the new attorneys and the remnants of Thrumburt's crew were sitting in jail. Including Limpy Cop who was also charged with first-degree burglary, several counts of aggravated assault and kidnapping and numerous counts of destruction of property for the damage to her house and Sean's truck.

Even if Erren didn't want to see her, she'd gone to the trouble of retrieving his motorcycle from impound. It sat in her garage waiting. Just like she sat at home…waiting. She'd asked about him at the DEA and had been told there were no agents by that name. She'd even tried to trace who owned the lake property. Just another dead end.

Where is this new guy? She looked at her watch and knew she wouldn't be waiting much longer. She was missing Michael's first day home. He'd been released from the hospital and her father had steaks, Coronas and a recorded Cowboys game. Captain's orders or no, five more minutes and she was headed home.

A knock drew her attention to the open door. She stood, straightening the front of her shirt.

When she turned to introduce herself to Pike's replacement, there he was. Agent Erren Rhodes. Full Dallas P.D. uniform—from the hat under his arm to his shiny black shoes.

"Hello, Darby."

Whoa. Was that her heart dropping to her toes? She wanted to run to him, throw herself into his arms. But it had been three weeks without a peep. If he'd cared about her at all, wouldn't he have at least said goodbye?

Nothing since the warehouse, and he chose now to appear in her office doorway. She took a step toward him. Wanting to kiss the smile off his lips. Restraining herself from doing that, too.

"You have the most incredibly bad timing. Why are you impersonating a police officer? You have to get out of here. Now. I'm expecting my new boss."

She turned him toward the door, but he kept turning,

making a three-sixty to face her again. A uniform was definitely a way to blend in, but she had to get him out of there. Pronto.

What if he were caught? Did he have any trustworthy contacts left in the DEA?

What am I thinking? He's not a criminal. He's one of Pike's men. He's the man I love...

Oh, God, I really do love him!

"I'm in uniform because I'm a cop, Darby. I always have been," he said. "I really am a cop." He walked to Pike's desk, setting down his hat.

"I don't believe you." He was terrific liar.

Even his name tag said Rhodes. His hair was regulation-length short. She'd thought he'd been handsome with the bruises, but now with his clean-shaven face and deep tan he looked gorgeous. Hopefully, his dagger was still on a chain under his uniform.

"I quit the DEA and came back to the force. It took time to get all the paperwork approved and records in place that put my cover in jail. I put more than my share of people behind bars over the last six years. They didn't want the drug lords in south Texas to know where I decided to settle."

He definitely had a convincing story, but she wouldn't fall for it. He could tell whopper lies with a straight face.

"I can't name all the laws you've broken by impersonating an officer." She shoved the door shut with a little too much force. "If you'll give me a few minutes, I can pawn Pike's replacement off on someone, then I should be free to leave. Can you wait?"

"Unfortunately, no. I—"

"Oh." The disappointment she'd swallowed each time she'd hit a dead end trying to discover his identity crept into her throat.

"I have an appointment. Since I don't officially start until next week, the captain said I could come by later. Your dad said you couldn't make it this afternoon."

"How did you know?" She stomped down the part of her that wanted to believe. Smashed whatever made her want to jump to the conclusion he was taking Pike's place and that's why he was in her office. "Oh, you are thorough, I'll give you that."

"Darby…"

She watched his chest expand and waited for the release. "Are you… Are you holding your breath?" She was afraid to ask. Afraid of the answer.

Erren quickly exhaled, slightly shaking his head.

"Oh, my God. It's true. You really are working here?"

"That's what I've been trying to tell you." He moved around the corner of Pike's desk, planting himself on the edge of hers and fiddling with the amber paperweight. Each time he tossed it in the air, she imagined him tossing her heart from one hand to the other. Yes, melodramatic and severely over the top…but she had an excuse—she loved the guy.

"I heard your brother's awake. Sometime last week?" He set the chunk of amber down on her desk.

"Yeah, he woke up like nothing was wrong, surprised that he was in the hospital. But he remembers that Knighton shot him and Walter," she said.

"We know that Knighton was following your brother. We can only assume he didn't know what he'd stumbled upon until he told Thrumburt. It just snowballed from there when I started asking questions."

She tried to focus on what he was saying. But her heart was screaming for him to acknowledge her. How could he just sit there and talk about the case? How would she work with him across the room if he acted like a partner?

"So…you gave up the excitement of undercover work for this mundane job teaching cadets?"

Erren looked out the window at cadets on the training course. Every inch of him was uncomfortable. Had he misread her feelings that much? Hell, he thought she'd at least say how much she'd missed him. Sure as the sun rose he'd missed her. She'd been on his mind every passing minute of his exile at the FBI safe house.

She'd kept a cool head and a noncaring attitude since he'd arrived, but Erren could see through her. Yeah, Darby had learned how to lie in the last three weeks. But not well enough. She may have his tell down pat, but he knew hers, too.

"Sort of." He shrugged.

"More mystery?" She shrugged back.

Erren recognized the same attitude in the movement they'd both utilized. Ambivalence, the shrug he used to cover what he didn't want to say aloud. She had it down to perfection, making his read of her more difficult. "They brought me in to lead a special task force. The higher-ups actually suggested you'd be perfect to work with."

"But?"

"I didn't think it would be a good idea." Trying to tease her, he'd mistakenly hurt her again, hitting her where she was most vulnerable…her lack of confidence in herself.

"Right. I don't take orders well enough. I rush in and muck up undercover operations. I can just imagine what type of recommendation you'd give me."

"I don't think you do. You're perfect for the job. I thought we'd keep Pike's operation going…working together, but…" He watched her bite her lip but keep her face emotionless, like a cop listening intently. "But I think the department frowns on officers dating. So I'll need to transfer to a different division." He caught himself holding his breath and wanted to risk everything. He said what he'd wanted to ever since seeing her behind that desk. "I really want to kiss you, Darby."

He reached for her hand, desperate to touch her, but she avoided him.

"It's an interesting offer."

Which one?

"But I don't think you're being completely honest." She poked him in his abdomen and grinned. "I asked Michael about how he lived. He swore he never sold drugs or paid his rent with drug money and that Pike gave him everything he needed. How could the man afford to support my brother?"

"Well, he…um… He didn't actually pay for anything."

"I'm not following." She frowned.

"It was me. Don't get the wrong idea. I mean, I'm not old-money wealthy or anything."

"What? You're not Bruce Wayne?"

"I have a trust fund that provided what Pike needed to make this operation work." He slipped his hand around her waist but she avoided his grasp.

"Spill it, mister. No more secrets."

Darby stepped closer to him, tapping his name plate. The name that clearly read Rhodes. "I know that's not real. I've called in favors, took advantage of my celebrity status and run searches in every database law enforcement has to offer. Erren Rhodes does not exist."

"I'm standing right in front of you, O'Malley."

Capturing her hand in his, Erren pulled her to his chest and enclosed her arms within his. He tilted her chin back with the tip of his finger until he could see the emerald sparkle of her eyes.

"Be honest, you've got a thing for me, right?"

She nodded and raised her lips to his.

He gave away his heart in the kiss and never wanted it back. Darby was the woman he'd never allowed himself to imagine.

"So who are you really, cowboy?"

Before he answered, he waited for the slender quizzical arch of her brow that he adored. "Just the guy who loves you."

* * * * *

INTRIGUE

COMING NEXT MONTH

Available March 8, 2011

USA TODAY *bestselling author Lynne Graham*
is back with a thrilling new trilogy
SECRETLY PREGNANT, CONVENIENTLY WED

Three heroines must marry alpha males to keep
their dreams...but Alejandro, Angelo and Cesario
are not about to be tamed!

Book 1—JEMIMA'S SECRET
Available March 2011 from Harlequin Presents®.

JEMIMA yanked open a drawer in the sideboard to find
Alfie's birth certificate. Her son was her husband's child.
It was a question of telling the truth whether she liked it or
not. She extended the certificate to Alejandro.

"This has to be nonsense," Alejandro asserted.

"Well, if you can find some other way of explaining how
I managed to give birth by that date and Alfie not be yours,
I'd like to hear it," Jemima challenged.

Alejandro glanced up, golden eyes bright as blades and
as dangerous. "All this proves is that you must still have
been pregnant when you walked out on our marriage. It
does not automatically follow that the child is mine."

"'I know it doesn't suit you to hear this news now and I
really didn't want to tell you. But I can't lie to you about it.
Someday Alfie may want to look you up and get acquainted."

"If what you have just told me is the truth, if that little
boy does prove to be mine, it was vindictive and extremely
selfish of you to leave me in ignorance!"

Jemima paled. "When I left you, I had no idea that I was
still pregnant."

"Two years is a long period of time, yet you made no
attempt to inform me that I might be a father. I will want
DNA tests to confirm your claim before I make any deci-

sion about what I want to do."

"Do as you like," she told him curtly. "*I* know who Alfie's father is and there has never been any doubt of his identity."

"I will make arrangements for the tests to be carried out and I will see you again when the result is available," Alejandro drawled with lashings of dark Spanish masculine reserve.

"I'll contact a solicitor and start the divorce," Jemima proffered in turn.

Alejandro's eyes narrowed in a piercing scrutiny that made her uncomfortable. "It would be foolish to do anything before we have that DNA result."

"I disagree," Jemima flashed back. "I should have applied for a divorce the minute I left you!"

Alejandro quirked an ebony brow. "And why didn't you?"

Jemima dealt him a fulminating glance but said nothing, merely moving past him to open her front door in a blunt invitation for him to leave.

"I'll be in touch," he delivered on the doorstep.

What is Alejandro's next move? Perhaps rekindling their marriage is the only solution! But will Jemima agree?

*Find out in Lynne Graham's
exciting new romance
JEMIMA'S SECRET*

*Available March 2011
from Harlequin Presents®.*

Start your Best Body today with these top 3 nutrition tips!

1. SHOP THE PERIMETER OF THE GROCERY STORE: The good stuff—fruits, veggies, lean proteins and dairy—always line the outer edges of the store. When you veer into the center aisles, you enter the temptation zone, where the unhealthy foods live.

2. WATCH PORTION SIZES: Most portion sizes in restaurants are nearly twice the size of a true serving and at home, it's easy to "clean your plate." Use these easy serving guidelines:
- Protein: the palm of your hand
- Grains or Fruit: a cup of your hand
- Veggies: the palm of two open hands

3. USE THE RAINBOW RULE FOR PRODUCE: Your produce drawers should be filled with every color of fruits and vegetables. The greater the variety, the more vitamins and other nutrients you add to your diet.

Find these and many more helpful tips in

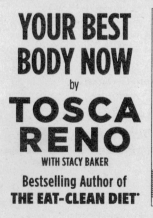

YOUR BEST BODY NOW
by
TOSCA RENO
WITH STACY BAKER

**Bestselling Author of
THE EAT-CLEAN DIET®**

Available wherever books are sold!